RITUAL HUMAN SACRIFICE

C.V. HUNT

GRINDHOUSE PRESS

Other Titles by C.V. Hunt

How To Kill Yourself

Zombieville

Thanks For Ruining My Life

Other People's Shit

Baby Hater

Hell's Waiting Room

Misery and Death and Everything Depressing

"Love is one of the most intense feelings felt by man; another is hate."

—Anton Szandor LaVey, *The Satanic Bible*

"Hell is empty, and all the devils are here."

—William Shakespeare, *The Tempest*

This novel was influenced by the writing of Bret Easton Ellis and Bentley Little.

Thank you

To Teresa Pollack, for reading this filth before anyone else. I thought about spelling your name wrong on purpose.

For Andy

I think our minds are twisted in the same direction.

PART 1

THE PREPARATION

1

This wasn't going to be easy. I'd played with the idea for the last year. And I'd been looking at apartments in the city close to my job for the last two months. Each night I would wait until Eve was asleep before spending hours scouring photos of potential apartments online. It was easy to use my job as an excuse to stay in the study and screw around on the computer. I told Eve I was working on a blueprint for a top client. But in actuality I was researching a new place to live . . . without her.

I masturbated to free internet porn whenever I wasn't searching one of the local realtor's sites for a new place. It felt like I was stalling and trying to find excuses not to move. But I wanted a place that wouldn't make me more depressed than I already was. This meant digging through photos of shitty apartments or driving by to check out their locations.

Besides, nightly masturbation was my preferred method of orgasm and I used it regularly to clear my head. Jerking off was cleaner than sex, drier, and the aftermath was completely disposable. I could shoot my load into a tissue and wash my hands. That was it. It was over and I could get back to more important things. There wasn't time wasted on showering afterward and the result was the same.

When I stopped to think about what went wrong between Eve and me the only conclusion I came to was our sex life had grown stale and boring. Comfortability and familiarity were relationship killers. Once you were comfortable with another person sex became repetitious and predictable and boring. You let your guard slip and you were stuck doing missionary for the next thirty years or until one of you fell over dead. Sex became something you did to pass the time or get rid of a headache or to break up the monotony of the day but it was as exciting as taking out the trash. At thirty-eight years old I might have been old but I wasn't dead. And I thought since Eve recently turned thirty her sex drive might pick up. It had. But Eve's idea of sex was mechanical and forced. There wasn't any excitement in the act anymore. There wasn't any foreplay. It was cold and over. Which didn't bother me much but there were the minutes wasted washing off the shame of complacency and her juices and the copious amount of lube she used now. The whole act of sex felt like a sticky chore and a bother and slightly disgusting. I was sure I could stir more emotion and enthusiasm out of a prostitute. Whenever I jerked off to an artificial and surgically enhanced girl on the internet I debated whether or not it would be worth the money and trouble and potential jail time to hire one. But I knew I would never do it because I would be too paranoid about catching a disease even if I did use a condom.

Eve sat across from me and ate her dinner in silence. She pinched a piece of fried chicken between her thumb and forefinger and raked her fork across the meat until some dislodged. She stabbed the meat and lifted it to her mouth, still holding the greasy chicken with her fingers. I could feel myself grimace. I couldn't understand why she didn't eat the damn thing with both of her hands like a barbarian.

Aside from her inability to eat like a lady she was attractive. Her blond hair was shorter than when I first met her eight years ago. We'd met when she was a fresh college graduate. She was cute and quirky then. She used to wear her hair in a messy ponytail and sported jeans and T-shirts for every occasion. There was something about her messiness when she was younger that was attractive and carefree. But once she started her job as an elementary teacher the cute college girl gear went into thrift store donation boxes. She cut and styled her hair into something more manageable or, as she put it, a style she didn't have to spend too much time on. And pant suits became her uniform. Eve was by no means hideous with the school teacher makeover but the free-spirited part of her was tossed out with her jeans and hair ties. She became pensive and serious. So when she threw those things out my level of excitement in her dropped. She wasn't the girl I'd met and originally fallen in love with. Everything about her became clinical and sterile. And my attitude about the sloppiness changed too. I grew to want things cleaner. Including her.

Eve chewed slowly and watched me. A glimmer of concern washed across her face. She started to open her mouth to say something but thought better about talking with her mouth full. I thanked her silently to myself. I hated repeating myself and sounding like a broken record whenever I pointed out general courtesies . . . like talking with your mouth full.

She said, "Is the food all right?"

"Yes," I said. "It's very good."

"You've hardly touched it."

I looked down at my plate and pushed the potatoes around with my fork. It dawned on me the potatoes were a recipe she rarely used anymore. She only made them on special occasions.

"Sorry," I said. "It's a nice dinner. Thank you for making it. I've got a lot on my mind."

"Me too." She smiled hesitantly.

I took a tentative bite of the potatoes. Ever since I started searching for an apartment my stomach hadn't felt well. It wasn't when I began looking for apartments my stomach went to shit though. It was when I realized why I was looking for apartments. My stomach went sour when I knew without a doubt the only way to keep my sanity was to leave Eve.

Eve complained about how small my apartment was the day she moved in. She'd had too much stuff and tried to cram it in next to mine. Eventually she sold all of my furniture because she thought hers was more stylish. Her furniture looked like it previously belonged to an old woman or was picked up from a bedbug riddled thrift store. My skin still crawled whenever I sat on the sofa. And once she hung all the knick-knacks and shelves on the walls I felt I was living in my grandmother's house minus the abundant amount of cigarette smoke and the mothball smell. Eve thought my modern furnishings were cold and sad and lacked character. She said architects weren't interior decorators and I let her do whatever she wanted to keep her happy even though I hated it.

I thought, *I should've put all of my furniture in storage instead of letting Eve sell everything.* I was going to have to buy all new stuff. At least I would get to choose everything *I* liked. I could go back to my modern and minimal existence. And everything would be new and clean and sterile. I wouldn't have to worry about a flea infestation or think about how someone else might have sat on my sofa with their bare ass. My mind reeled at the thought of everything else that could have happened on it.

I chewed a bite of potatoes and stared at my plate.

"Nick?" she said.

"Hm." I looked up at her.

She wrung her napkin. She gripped the material so hard her knuckles were white. I could see a sheen of grease from the chicken on her index finger. Why wouldn't she use the fork to hold the chicken and a knife to cut it? Did she like the way it felt when her teeth nicked the bone? Did she like the feel of the warm tendons pinched between her fingers?

She said, "Did you hear me?"

I swallowed my food and stabbed another piece of potato. I stared at her and tried to come up with a better excuse than I had a lot on my mind.

In a gush she repeated what I hadn't heard while I was lost in thought. "I'm pregnant."

My heart came to a screeching halt. Numbness spread throughout my entire body and I felt ungrounded. I dropped my fork. It bounced off the table and clattered across the floor. The potato speared on the tines soared toward the ceiling, arched, and landed on the table between the two of us.

My heart slammed back into gear and hammered against my ribs. I blinked and wondered if my ticker was up for this kind of trauma.

Eve ignored the contaminated fork and food. Her eyes bounced back and forth, searching mine for an answer to a question she hadn't asked.

A million questions and scenarios raced through my head at once. I wasn't sure how to respond. I wasn't even sure if I was here in the kitchen with her anymore. My body was going to float away at any moment because this had to be a dream. The connecting strings of gravity felt severed. I prayed I'd had a heart attack from her announcement and was dead and my spirit still sat in my chair staring at Eve and I was feeling the phantom sensations of living. But I knew I couldn't be that lucky. This wasn't a dream. I wasn't dead. And the latter would've been preferable.

When Eve and I met I told her I didn't want to be a father. I was the only child of a couple who didn't want children. Some people would call my situation an unplanned pregnancy. I knew I was an accident. I'm sure if my parents would have had the money or the knowledge of where to go they would've aborted me the moment my mother knew she was pregnant.

To say my parents were shitty parents was an understatement. They didn't nurture or support me in any form because they never wanted me. I knew if I had children I would end up being a shitty parent too. I didn't want to be the asshole to an undeserving victim of circumstance. Eve agreed she didn't want children either when we'd first met. We flirted with the subject briefly after we'd gotten married and she'd said she was content with dealing with a classroom full of kids through the week and enjoying the quiet weekends to herself. And I didn't argue with her because she already knew my thoughts about having children.

I ran all these things over and over in my head. How could this have happened to us? I was almost forty. I couldn't start a family now. Eve was thirty. Weren't there supposed to be more complications for older women? Wasn't there a higher risk of birth defects? Was she going to give birth to a Down syndrome kid? Wasn't that what happened to women who had children later in life?

Eve's words slapped me back into reality. "Nick . . . say something."

I blurted out the two worst sentences a man in my position could. "Oh no," and, "We can get it taken care of."

Eve's expression shifted to appalled in a blink of an eye. "Taken care of?"

"Well . . . you know . . ."

She smacked her fork down on the table. The loud *clack* of the metal against wood sounded like a gunshot in our tiny apartment. I flinched.

She leaned forward and furrowed her brow. "Why would you think I want an abortion?"

My ears tingled. I wasn't sure if it was from shock or embarrassment. "Because we've always said we didn't want children."

"*You've* always said *you* didn't want children."

"Excuse me? You said you dealt with screaming brats every day and you didn't want one at home."

"I never called them brats."

"Wait a minute," I said. I closed my eyes and pinched my brow. I wished there was something I could do to scramble and reset my thoughts. I wanted to blur the chaos inside my head like the small pieces of plastic inside a snow globe so maybe they would slowly settle into a serene scene again and I could focus. I opened my eyes. Eve leaned back in her chair, folded her arms, and gave me a venomous look. I ran the tips of my fingers along my eyebrow and tried to dispel the tension headache building there. A thought struck me. I dropped my hands to the table. Her hard demeanor wavered and I caught an edge of nervousness.

I said, "Please don't tell me you got pregnant on purpose."
Her expression shifted. She lifted an eyebrow and appeared arrogant when she responded. "I did."
I took a deep breath and tried to sound calm. "Why would you do that?"
"Because you would've said no if I'd asked."
"You're fuckin' right I would've."
She uncrossed her arms and smiled. "People only *say* they don't want children. But what they really mean is they don't want children at that time." She waited for a few seconds before continuing, "I'm not getting any younger. I didn't have time to debate with you for another eight years."
"There wouldn't have been a debate. The answer was always no. The answer *is* no."
Eve sighed and picked up her fork. "It's too late now. What's done is done."
I wanted to scream at her. I wanted to rip out my receding shoulder length hair. I wanted to verbally attack her and tell her I was seconds away from leaving her before she dropped this atomic bomb. I wanted her to regret sabotaging me and force her to get up from the table and walk out the door. I wanted to tell her to have fun raising the little shit by herself. I wanted to go to a bar and get drunk and pick up a young hot girl and take her to a hotel and fuck the shit out of her to release my aggressions so I could come home and tell Eve I'd had an affair so she would kick me out. I wanted to fuck her life over the way she'd fucked mine over. I wanted her to be as angry and frustrated with me as much as I was with her. I wanted to see her cry.
I ground my teeth as she ate. She chose to ignore me and my impeccable ability to restrain myself from exploding by paying close attention to the food on her plate. My left eye twitched. My ears rang. I prayed for a stroke.
I took a deep breath and let it out slowly. I said, "You think this city and its school systems are a great place to raise a kid?"
She swallowed her food and tilted her head to the side. "Is

that some sort of backhanded insult directed at my teaching ability?"

It was. But I wasn't going to say that. "No. I'm stating the obvious. This city is overrun with violent crimes and the schools don't rank highly for the state. I thought it might've been something you mulled over before deciding to have a child. Most people would take the next eighteen years into consideration."

She sighed and got up from the table. She sauntered toward me and forced herself between me and the table and sat on my lap. I was a statue. I refused to touch her. She wrapped her arms around me and spoke close to my face. Her breath smelled of chicken grease. I wasn't sure if it was the revulsion of her breath or the situation making me want to push her off my lap. I wanted to push her so hard she fell to the floor.

"It's going to be okay," she said. "These things have a way of working themselves out. If everyone thought about every miniscule detail of how their children's lives may or may not work out no one would have children."

I thought, *Only rational and smart people wouldn't have children. Morons would still keep reproducing and hope the world would be filled with pixie dust and fairy godmothers to fix everything.*

I refused to meet her gaze and stared at her empty chair across the table. I held my breath when she spoke so I didn't have to breathe in hers. My tolerance for stupidity had drastically decreased over time and this may have been the stupidest situation I'd ever been in.

She said, "You're only mad because you don't think you can do this. But I know you can. I know you better than anyone else."

I thought, *If you know me so well why didn't you know I was seconds from leaving you? And you make me miserable.*

"Every new dad has the jitters," she said. "Believe me, I've read a lot of stories about it. Your nurturing instinct will kick in once the baby's here and you'll be glad we did this."

We? I thought. *There was definitely no we in this situation. Why would you ever think I would eventually be ecstatic when a squirming hunk of flesh that oozes snot, tears, vomit, piss, and shit arrived in my house and assaulted my senses every second of every day?*

"It'll be like getting a surprise gift you never knew you wanted."

I clenched my jaw. I wanted to say all of the things I was thinking. But I knew if I opened my mouth to speak I would leak every venomous thought I'd ever had of her. I would say evil things. I would say hurtful things. I would say things a million years and a billion apologies would never erase.

"Will you say something?" she said.

I finally looked at her. "What do you want me to say?"

"I don't know. Anything. Anything would be better than nothing. Jesus . . . I'd rather you bitch me out right now than sit there like a lump."

I could have said I knew everything would be okay and pretended to be happy. But I wanted to be pissed. Maybe if I upset her enough she would kick me out. Then I wouldn't be at fault. I wouldn't have walked out on my pregnant wife; she would have thrown me out. I would still be an asshole but not as big of an asshole as some guy who left his wife after she told him she was having his child.

"Okay," I said. "How about I say thanks for making a major life decision for me without consulting me? How about I say, and you know it too, our marriage isn't perfect and bringing a child into it isn't going to fix it?"

Eve's happy demeanor collapsed and she stood up. "You're an ass!" she hissed.

She picked up my plate and dumped my food in the sink. She turned on the water and garbage disposal.

I yelled over the noise, "Well, our kid is going to be half ass and half selfish control freak!"

She turned the disposal off and faced me. Tears streamed down her face. She said, "Could you be a normal person and actually give a shit you're going to be a father?"

"I give a shit. It's just not exactly how you want me to give a shit. How would you feel if I made a major life decision for the both of us without telling you until it was said and done?"

She wiped the tears from her face. Her nose and eyes were red and her cheeks were blotchy. Eve was not a pretty crier.

She said, "I wouldn't care because I know you would make the right decision. Whatever you were deciding would be something for the better. It would be for the both of us and it would be an improvement."

"Do you really think having a child is going to improve our situation?"

"I do."

"How?"

"We'll be a family."

"We're a family now."

She crossed her arms and leaned back against the counter. "No. Right now we're a couple. There's a difference. There's a huge difference."

"Yeah, another human being. One that requires more money, more food, more healthcare, more attention." I counted the list on my fingers as I spoke. "God knows how you're going to shrivel up and die when half of my attention is redirected to another human being."

She glared at me and spoke through clenched teeth. "Please don't make me say fuck you." She closed her eyes and took a deep breath. When she opened her eyes she was calm. The blotchiness of her skin was replaced with a flush of anger. "There's no sense in arguing about this all night. It is what it is."

I got up from the table and collected her plate. I took it to the sink and dumped the food in and switched on the disposal. Eve still leaned her butt against the counter beside the sink. She placed the heels of her palms on the counter to either side of her. She watched me as I did the dishes and put them in the drying rack. When I was finished I walked toward the living area.

"Nick."

I stopped in the doorway between the kitchen and living room and turned to her. She stared at me as if she'd asked a question. I raised an eyebrow as if to ask what she wanted.

"That's it then?" she said.

I shrugged. "There's no sense in arguing about it all night, right? You've made up our minds for us."

She huffed as I turned to walk away. I stopped again and turned back to her.

"By the way," I said. "I'm going to pretend I'm happy about this around friends and family. I'm going to pretend everything is okay between us. I'm willing to wait and see if this is what we really need. On the inside I'm seething right now." I spread the sarcasm on thick. "But, hey, maybe you're right. Maybe this kid comes along and turns the lion into a lamb and all of a sudden everything is right in the world and the baby cleans the cobwebs out of our marriage. Hey, cleaning up baby shit at three A.M. might boost our sex life. But overall, I'm going to be the happiest father to be on the planet. I'm going to help out and buy ice cream late at night. I'll go to whatever parties you throw for your stretch marked belly. I'll do it all in exchange for one thing."

She appeared crestfallen and on the verge of tears. I'd wanted her to cry and succeeded in provoking the tears but I couldn't stomach watching her bawl all night. Her blotchy and scrunched face was beginning to annoy me. She brought this upon herself and could cry all she wanted. But crying was not going to get her what she wanted. I wanted to walk away and drop the bargaining bit but knew she would follow me and interrogate me which was more annoying than watching her cry.

She replied hesitantly, "In exchange for what?"

"You can't get pissed when I make huge decisions affecting both our lives without your consent."

"I won't." She replied without hesitation.

I smiled at her jovially and walked into our tiny living room. I cringed when I sat on the possibly diseased sofa and picked up the television remote and clicked the power button.

2

My office was very modern. A glass wall separated me from the rest of the office. Sometimes I would stare at the others as they worked while I tried to envision a project. Today I was mesmerized by Sadie as she filed some paperwork in a row of stainless steel cabinets. I wasn't staring at Sadie because she was attractive. It was the exact opposite. Her appearance was lumpy and repulsive and she was old enough to be my mother. It didn't seem possible for a human body to be shaped like hers and I spent an embarrassing amount of time trying to decipher how she'd managed to morph herself into her current state. She looked like Mrs. Santa Claus. Or what Mrs. Claus would look like if she wore shirts with photos of cats and quirky quotes printed on them with elastic banded jeans and sandals. I never could understand the sandals. They were the main focus of my attention. It didn't matter what time of year it was, rain or snow, she always wore those damn busted down sandals without any socks. Our office didn't have a dress code and some days I wished it did.

Sadie's feet were a sight to behold. They were dry and flaky and cracked. Horrendous elephant feet. I couldn't stop staring at them whenever she was around. Someday I would stare at her feet and a large chunk of crusted skin would peel off and land on the floor. Or worse yet, someone would catch me staring at her feet and think I had some sort of crusty foot or granny fetish. If I was accused of either of those things I would quit.

There were times when I fantasized about sneaking a Ped Egg into her cubicle and leaving it on her desk while she was at lunch. Maybe I would throw in a pair of tennis shoes. But she wasn't competent enough to know you should wash your tennis shoes after every wear and they'd end up transforming into something funky like her feet. The shoes might even exacerbate her foot condition. The thought made me cringe.

Eve thought I was insane for washing my tennis shoes after each wear. She said washing your shoes warped them and was weird. I kept several pairs and found if you washed them and let them air dry it didn't destroy the integrity of the construction. Eve still refused to wash her filthy shoes. God only knew what her feet would end up looking like.

Sadie moved to her cubicle where I couldn't see her. I redirected my attention to my computer monitor. I'd spent most of the morning putting the final touches on a design for a client. My specialty was office buildings. They were a cinch. Most of the clients in the market for these types of buildings wanted approximately the same thing: vast, tall, clean lines, modern, stone, tile, and glass. These clients were my people. They understood a building could be a modern work of art. I hardly thought twice about the design as I drafted.

When I was finished I emailed the files to Mr. Crutch for review. I checked the clock. It was fifteen minutes till lunch. Sam from Human Resources walked past my open office door. I called for him. In one fluid motion he pivoted on his heel and poked his head through the doorway.

"What's up?" he said.

"Do you have a minute?"

"Sure," he said cheerfully.

"Could you close the door?" I said.

He stepped in, shut the door, and took a seat across from me.

Sam wore dress clothes even though he didn't have to.

Most of his outfits consisted of simple button down shirts and dress pants. His clothes were always a shade of dark gray or black. He never fussed with a tie. There was something about the simplicity of gray and black I found stylish. Sam was ten years younger than I and was enthusiastic and easygoing. I secretly wanted to copy his style but thought it would be too strange and *Single White Female*. I stuck to my black or gray T-shirts with no logos, designer jeans, and tennis shoes. I liked the idea of being a blank slate in case a client popped in with some last minute changes or questions. Clients rarely stopped in but it never hurt to keep the average guy appearance.

Sam crossed his legs in an effeminate manner. "What's up?"

"I have a few questions and I wasn't sure who to ask."

"Okay." He pointed his finger at me as if his hand were a gun. "Fire away."

"What's our policy on confidentiality?"

Sam's perpetual smile wavered and he appeared worried. "It's that bad?" He waved his hand dismissively. "Anything you say stays with me unless it needs to be redirected to another department." He uncrossed his legs and folded his hands in his lap. "You've worked here long enough to know Mr. Crutch doesn't like gossip."

"Fair enough." I tried to relax. "What's our policy on paternity leave?"

Sam raised his eyebrows. He made a noise that sounded like a mixture of a hiccup and a gasp. "Oh my god!" he said a tad too loud.

Through the window I spotted Sadie's head peek from behind her cubicle wall. She stared in our direction.

I motioned discretely with my hand for Sam to keep his voice down. "Sadie is watching."

Sam stared at me with a shocked expression. He covered his mouth and feigned a boisterous cough to insinuate any loud noises from our direction were a coughing jag on his part. He whispered, "Sorry." He dropped his hand from his mouth.

"You know the office people," I said. "I don't want them to know yet. They always want some reason to make cake. It's too soon to celebrate."

"Not far along?"

"No."

Sadie didn't bother to hide her overt curiosity and continued to stare. I made eye contact with her and she dropped back behind her cubicle wall.

Sam said, "I didn't think you guys could have children. Not that it's any of my business."

I didn't know how to respond to him. We could've had a child at any time. Eve was the one who hadn't held up her end of the bargain. I didn't know how to explain it to Sam. He was a nice guy but we didn't know each other beyond work. To tell him what happened was awkward. It was privy information you shared with a personal friend or family. Telling people you never wanted to have children was a touchy subject.

An awkward silence enveloped the room. I panicked and racked my brain to find the proper way to answer him.

"I'm sorry," Sam said, "you don't have to go into details." His cheeks flushed and he backpedaled. "Don't listen to me. I'm an idiot."

"It's okay."

"You wanted to know about paternity leave?"

"Yes."

"It's six weeks. You can choose to take it however you like. Most guys will take one to two weeks before the birth and the remainder after. The pay is sixty percent of your regular salary. Or you can choose to continue to work from home and receive a hundred percent."

"That's another question . . . Do we have a policy for working at home full-time?"

He furrowed his brow. "I don't think we do. Probably because it's never come up."

"Ninety-nine percent of my job can be done from home. And all of my work is done on a computer and through email. It's rare for me to actually meet a client. When I do it's by appointment . . . which I could come in for."

Sam nodded his head while I listed the key points of my case. "I understand. William worked from home after his son was born. I don't remember any major issues."

"Who would I ask about working from home full-time?"

He leaned back in the chair, laced his fingers behind his head, and squinted at the ceiling as though the answer were printed there. "I guess Mr. Crutch." He redirected his gaze to me. "The company's a sole proprietorship. He pretty much makes whatever policies he wants as long as he sticks within the law. I could run it by him and see what he has to say."

"That would be great," I said. "I'd still come in for the monthly meetings. And I'll be here to meet with clients upon request. If he seems hesitant tell him I'm willing to take a ten percent pay cut."

"You want this pretty bad, huh?" He unlaced his fingers and rested his hands in his lap.

"Like you wouldn't believe." I smiled.

"So, you're gonna be a stay-at-home dad?"

"That's the plan."

"That's cool. You don't see that as often as the moms." He stared at my name plate for a second and smiled as if he'd thought of something. "Eve's a lucky gal."

"I appreciate your help."

"Is there a certain date you're looking to start?"

The traffic of coworkers passing my office increased and I knew it was lunch time.

"No. I've got a few months."

"Okay. Good. That gives me time to ease it on Mr. Crutch. Personally, I don't see any problem. I'd let you do it in a heartbeat if it were up to me, but ultimately, it's his decision."

He slapped the arms of the chair lightly and stood. I stood with him. He extended his hand and I shook it.

"Congratulations," he said.

I pumped his hand a few times. "Thanks."

He released my hand and briskly left my office and headed toward his own. I sat down at my computer and stared at the monitor for a few seconds before I placed my hand on the mouse. I opened the internet search engine and typed in the word 'Realtor'.

3

I drove through the small town. It appeared to have the basic essentials: a post office, a grocery store with a sign advertising the only pharmacy was inside, a gas station, a hardware store, a doctor's office, a church, and a few dozen houses.

The town had one stoplight and it was probably more of a nuisance for people passing through than anything else. It was obvious Edenville wasn't a tourist destination. The only movement on the main street was a flag flapping lackadaisically in front of the post office. If the street light didn't work, and the buildings were more worn, the town would appear abandoned.

I followed the GPS's instructions and turned down a country road on the edge of town. Within a quarter of a mile I was engulfed in trees. There were a few breaks in the tree line for driveways. One could drive right by them without noticing them if it wasn't for the mailboxes. I peered down a few of the drives as I passed. I thought I could make out hints of houses hidden in the foliage.

After a few miles the GPS announced my upcoming destination on the right. I knew from the realtor's website most of the trees—with the exception of a few larger ones—were cleared from the front yard to give an unobstructed view of the road. I slowed the car when I spotted the gap in the trees and turned onto the gravel drive for the house.

An older model Oldsmobile was parked beside the house. I rolled toward it.

The pictures on the realtor's website didn't do the house justice. The structure was massive. Even after all my years of laying out floor plans and designing I couldn't wrap my head around square footage. I knew forty-five hundred square feet of living space was more than Eve and I would ever need but it was a much welcome upgrade. Our apartment was only nine hundred square feet. This house would give me and Eve space. Not space to grow but space to be separate from one another.

The house was three stories tall. Its appearance made me think a schizophrenic on acid designed and decorated it. The original structure must've been a modest two-story farmhouse but someone added a third floor and an addition on the opposite side of the drive. The addition was bigger than the house itself.

The materials used for the outside were a hodgepodge of aluminum siding and wooden clapboard. None of the pieces matched in color. Someone used green corrugated plastic to cover a section toward the front of the house. And the addition looked as if they'd used parts of a boat to build it, including the helm. Random murals were painted on the house and most of them appeared to be Egyptian in nature.

I parked beside the Oldsmobile. I didn't see the realtor and assumed he was inside checking the house over before showing it. This was the best time to inspect the outside without someone leering over my shoulder.

I exited the car and was bombarded with the constant sound of crickets. The temperature was warm but I could smell the arrival of fall. There was a slight odor of decayed foliage. The nights had become cool the last couple of weeks. It wouldn't be long before the first frost and leaves began changing color. I surveyed the large yard and trees and imagined the area would be very colorful by the time we moved in.

I headed toward the front of the house and looked for

RITUALISTIC HUMAN SACRIFICE

signs of an unstable foundation. There were no cracks and no major erosion. Everything was in great shape for the age of the house.

A covered porch engulfed the front of the house. I climbed the stairs and bounced my weight to make sure the boards were sturdy. I approached the stained glass front door and was about to try the knob when I noticed markings on the doorframe. I leaned in for a closer inspection. The markings were symbols in faded brown paint along each side of the door. They also ran along the top and bottom of the jamb. It looked as if someone used their fingers to paint the characters.

I squinted at one of the symbols and tried to identify the picture. There was a finger print at the end of the brush stroke. I moved in closer and caught an awful scent that reminded me of menstrual blood and feces. I gagged, took a couple steps back, and covered my nose with my hand. The front door opened.

A middle-aged man stood in the doorway. He was the same height as me but his proportions were mammoth. He had a large head with dark, side swept hair, giving me the impression he was hiding a bald spot. He wore a windbreaker over a white button down shirt. The first few buttons of his shirt were unfastened. Gray chest hair peeked through the opening and I noted a gold chain around his neck. He took noisy breaths through his mouth.

He wore latex gloves and removed one with a snap and extended a meaty and hairy hand toward me. "Nick Graves?"

I dropped my hand from my nose and stared at his extended hand. I didn't know why he was wearing the gloves but I imagined it was because he recently finished handling something foul. I hesitated but thought it would be bad manners not to shake his hand. I extended my hand and cringed internally when he clasped it with his own sweaty one.

"Yes," I said.

"Jim Hagathorne," he said. "I thought I heard someone pull in."

He released my hand. I dropped my arm but held it out from my body a few inches. I didn't want to touch anything—especially anything on my body—until I had a chance to use the hand sanitizer in my car.

"I was looking around outside," I said.

Jim waved his ungloved hand in a beckoning motion and stepped out of the doorway. "Come in. Have a look around."

He pulled off the other glove and balled them together. He shoved the dirty gloves into the pocket of his windbreaker, followed by his hands. Internally I immediately nicknamed him 'The Walking Cesspool'.

I stepped past Jim and into an insanely large living room. The room had high ceilings with crown molding. Someone in the course of the house's history thought it was a good idea to paint the wood molding an awful maroon color. The walls were a faded sunshine yellow and the floors were covered with worn and stained hunter green carpet. I could smell cat piss and knew what the stains on the carpet were. An open staircase was situated on the far left of the room. A doorway beside the stairs led to a poorly decorated den. The stair banister was a nice dark wood but the stairs themselves were covered with tacky Berber carpet. I sighed internally at people's poor taste.

The only thing salvageable in the living area was a large fireplace made of gray stone. At least someone hadn't painted the stones. Nothing irritated me more than painted stone or brick.

"It's a lot of house for the money," Jim said.

I ignored him and walked toward the kitchen. The floor squeaked beneath my feet and I knew the previous owner committed one of the worst crimes against any great structure—they'd carpeted over the hardwood floors. I stepped through the large archway to the kitchen and found it was also hideously decorated. I'd hoped from the pictures I'd viewed online the countertops and cabinets were real wood. They were not. I sneered at the floral linoleum and checked the water flow in the second small sink located on the island.

RITUALISTIC HUMAN SACRIFICE

Someone had spaced the island awkwardly from the rest of the L-shaped kitchen. There seemed to be too much room and I wondered if the previous owners were obese.

Jim followed and watched me closely. I checked the water in the main sink and inspected under both sinks to make sure there were no leaks.

Jim pulled a folded piece of paper from his back pocket and opened it. He dug a pair of reading glasses out of his windbreaker pocket. When he removed the glasses one of the dirty latex gloves fell on the floor. The Walking Cesspool picked up the filthy glove and shoved it back into the pocket. He perched the glasses on the end of his nose and began to read from a list of features.

"Four-thousand five-hundred and two feet of living space. Four finished bedrooms on the second floor." He thumbed over his shoulder toward the living room. "A study off the living room." He pointed toward the two doors on the left side of the kitchen. "A laundry slash utility room, three full baths, a finished loft area on the third floor, and fifteen unfinished rooms in the addition."

I walked over to the two doors he motioned to and glanced in. One was a grimy bathroom in desperate need of a complete update. I checked the water, flushed the toilet, and looked under the sink.

The other room housed a furnace, water heater, and the hookups for a washer and dryer.

I stood in the doorway to the utility room and pointed at the water heater and furnace. "Do these work?"

Jim stared at the paper in his hand. "Says they both passed inspection and both are electric."

I walked to the back door and moved a dusty curtain to look out the window. There was a small screened porch attached to the back of the house. Beyond the porch lay a vast back yard and a wall of trees.

Jim thrust his large head over my shoulder to peer out the window. "Great view."

His breath smelled like Chipotle burritos. I stepped away

so he could admire the view and to take a breath not tainted with his essence.

He smiled like an imbecile as he looked out the window. He turned to me. "Want to check out the rest of the house?"

"Sure." I motioned for him to lead.

I followed him to the stairs. He commented on how structurally sound the house was. He asked if I noticed any sounds from outside. I hadn't noticed until he mentioned it but I couldn't hear anything from outside. And even if I wanted to hear the insects his noisy breathing made it hard to discern anything beyond the walls of the house. But there was an unusual vacuum-like quality to the structure. The air was thick and there was an almost unperceivable pressure on my eardrum. The sensation gave me the impression I was walking through gelatin filled space. I told him it was very quiet.

The stairs led to a wide hallway with three doors on each side. The second floor was entirely covered with an old floral pattern carpet with red and green hues. It reminded me of Christmas. Jim stepped repeatedly in one spot to produce a squeak from the floorboards. He made a remark about the floors being wood underneath the awful carpet. Each bedroom was painted a various shade of hideous color. And none of them matched the gross carpet. One room was pastel pink, another was metallic gold, and the last two were a dark and light shade of avocado green.

As advertised, there was a bathroom on the second floor. I entered it to check for any soft spots in the carpeted floor. The worst thing you could install in a bathroom was carpet. It retained water and caused the floor underneath to mold and rot. But the floor was solid. And I didn't detect any smell of mildew. The previous owner might not have used the shower on this level often.

The bathroom walls were tiled with pastel pink and blue tiles. The tub, toilet, and sink were coral colored ceramic. I didn't even bother checking the water. Everything was ugly and would have to go. If the contractors found a problem when they ripped it out it would be fixed then.

Jim stood in the doorway. "They had an eclectic taste in colors."

"The walls definitely need painted."

"Want to head up to the third floor?"

"Sure. From the pictures online, it looked like the only area I won't have to completely gut."

I followed him to last door on the right. It opened to an enclosed staircase. I ascended first. The stairs were made of a dark wood and the walls were white. It was the only part of the house I found aesthetically pleasing. The stairs led to a room as large as the second floor. The floors and ceiling were made of the same wood as the stairs. The walls were painted a soft matte white. A single modern chandelier hung from the center of the ceiling. The whole wall facing the back of the house was made of a series of floor to ceiling windows with a break in the middle for a set of French doors. I approached the doors and found a balcony overlooking the woods beyond the back yard.

"Wow," I said. "This is fantastic."

"I'm not sure what they used this room for," Jim said, "but it has a ballroom feel to it, don't ya think?"

I glanced around the room again and shrugged. I strolled across the floor and inspected it. Whoever lived here, and whatever they used this space for, they had taken good care of the floor. There were no gouges or scuffs in the finish.

A door was located beside the stairs. I opened it and found a stylish bathroom. Everything appeared in good working order.

"Okay," I said. "Show me the unfinished part."

"It's got a secret door," he said. He waved enthusiastically for me to follow him.

We headed down to the first floor in silence. At the bottom of the stairs on the ground level he rounded the stairs and stopped at a door I hadn't notice before. The door was painted matte black and blended into the shadows cast by the stairs.

Jim laid his hand on the knob and turned to me. All the

climbing up and down stairs had winded him and his mouth breathing was annoying. I took a step back from him so I wouldn't be subjected to his awful rotten breath.

He said, "I think the previous owner either had a pet they let run around in here or a wild animal somehow found a way into this part of the house. I tried to clean it up but the smell hasn't had time to air out."

I nodded. The house already smelled like cat piss. I couldn't imagine it could be much worse. He opened the door and the godawful stench emanating from within was overwhelming. A reek of wet dog and feces hung heavily in the air and assaulted my sinuses. The odor felt like a physical thing. It was oily and I cringed as I imagined it soaking into my clothes and my hair and my pores.

The odor wasn't the only thing unusual about the addition. I found myself standing in a hallway lined with doors. But the hallway wasn't straight. It zigzagged back and forth at forty-five degree angles. The walls were drywall but it wasn't taped or mudded. The floors were unfinished subflooring.

"Weird," I said. "There weren't any pictures of this on the site. I thought maybe it was in bad shape. It looks like they were close to finishing."

"The angles of the hall made it a pain to get photos. It's sort of hard to convey what's going on here. And the software only allows so many photos for each listing."

He closed the door we'd entered and pointed at it. A mirror was affixed to the back of the door. I shrugged. I didn't think it was a big deal. Mirrors weren't a selling point for me. Especially cheap ones you could pick up at any one stop shopping center.

"Superstition," he said.

"What do you mean?"

He smirked and waved his hand dismissively. "Some of us old timers are superstitious."

"A mirror is superstitious?"

"You're supposed to hang a mirror on the wall opposing your front door. It's meant to drive away evil spirits. Spirits are terrified of their own reflection and it keeps them from entering your home."

I inspected my reflection. I couldn't imagine how hideous I'd have to be to avoid my own reflection.

"It's a good thing I'm not superstitious," I said. "Besides . . . they have it in the wrong spot. "

I proceeded down the funhouse hall. The rooms were in the same state as the hallway: drywall, no tape or mud, sub-flooring, bare bulbs in the light fixtures. The jumbled construction of the outside had distracted me from noticing the addition had no windows.

Jim tagged along as I poked my head in each room and tried the light switch. In the last room on the first level I found a large dark stain on the floor. There was a tied trash bag beside it. I didn't think the stench could get any worse but it was apparent this room was ground zero. The bag contained a large solid mass.

Jim fidgeted and worry lines etched his face. I walked around the stain and stopped beside the bag. I didn't want to touch it. I knew whatever was in it was more than likely brimming with germs. But between the air, Jim's sweaty handshake and foul breath, and the few things I'd touched since being in the house, I would have to take a shower as soon as I got home. Besides, I washed my shoes after every wear. I gently toed the bag.

Jim waved his hands in a cautious manner. "Oh, don't do that."

"What's in it?"

"You don't want to know."

I eyed the bag and stain dubiously. I thought, *Even if this was scrubbed clean would the stench still be here?*

"Don't worry," Jim said. "If you decide you want to make an offer we can add a stipulation that the house be thoroughly cleaned before you move in."

I stared at him for a few uncomfortable seconds and hoped he would elaborate on the contents of the bag. He didn't. I saved my question for the end of the tour.

I left the room and found the stairs at the end of the hall. The second and third floors were the same design as the first: zigzagging hall and unfinished walls and floor. The smell was less cloying on the other floors. And there was no indication what the rooms were going to be used for. There were no plumbing fixtures in this part of the house. Jim trailed me and didn't say anything until we reached the end of the hall on the third floor.

"I'm not sure what they intended," he said. "My best guess is a wacky bed and breakfast."

"Maybe," I said. I peeked in the last room and turned to him. "Seems they would've added at least one bathroom per floor."

"At least there's plenty of room if it's something you had in mind. You could make some money on the side."

I shook my head. "I can't imagine a demand for a place to stay in Edenville. No . . . I just want a house for my family. I wouldn't be a good landlord."

He jokingly asked, "Do you have a big family?"

"No. But I really want this house."

He raised an eyebrow. "Starting a family?"

"One in the oven."

He gave me a toothy smile and shifted his massive weight from one foot to the other. "If you don't mind me asking . . . why this house? I have tons of others in the middle of nowhere if that's what you're looking for. They're in much better shape than this one." He waved his hand to insinuate the house. "You wouldn't have to drop a penny into them. Sure . . . they might cost more, but believe me, the money you would save not dealing with repairs, not to the mention the headache, you'd be a lot happier."

"To be blunt, I don't care for any of the other houses I've looked at. They're all three bedroom ranches with beige Berber carpet and beige walls and faux stone counter tops. They're nothing I haven't seen a million times in a million homes. They lack character."

Jim looked down the odd hallway and back to me. "This

place definitely has character."

"I'm sure there's nothing wrong with any of the other houses you'd show me and they'd make a great home for someone . . . but not for me."

"It sounds like you've already made up your mind. You sure you don't want to have the missus take a tour first?"

I understood why he was trying to steer me away from the house. His commission would be more with an expensive home. He wanted a bigger payday. He didn't want to be the object of gripes and groans when people asked which realtor I'd used. Overall he was looking out for his wallet and reputation.

But I wanted this house for several reasons. The house was unique and everything about it, before and after I remodeled it to my specifications—its location, the absence of a school—would infuriate Eve. She would have to give up her job as a teacher. I would work from home. She would homeschool our child. We would live at least two hours from any friends or family which meant I didn't have to pretend to be happy about the kid. But mostly, I was making a life decision that impacted both of us in a major way without her consent.

"No need." I waved my hand dismissively. "I'm buying the house. It's a surprise for my wife."

"I don't know how much of a surprise it will be. If you finance it stag she'll still have to sign a waiver at closing stating she's aware you're making a major purchase. It's one of those crazy laws so a spouse can't hide any assets from the other spouse in the event of a divorce." His face reddened and he backpedaled. "Not that you're going to get divorced—"

"Don't worry. The closing is when I plan on surprising her. We're expecting. She'll be thrilled to move out of our cramped apartment."

I knew Eve. She always complained about how crowded the apartment was. What she neglected to see was the place was claustrophobic because she owned too much stuff. If I sprung a new house on her she would be so excited she would sign the papers without question. If she did hesitate I would remind her I was allowed to make a major life decision for the both of us without consulting her. But what she wouldn't know when she signed the paper was that she was agreeing to completely uproot her life and flip it on its head. I felt it was only fair.

Jim said, "Does this mean you want to make an offer? Remember, its bank owned so the house is as-is. I could recommend an inspector if you'd like."

"No need. I know a lot of contractors who owe me favors."

He looked at his watch. "It'll take me forty-five minutes to get back to my office. I could fax the offer to them before they close. But you probably won't hear anything back for a day or two. You'd think the banks would want to get rid of these empty houses and get their money but they're really slow about responding. What about financing? You'll have to put down some earnest money if you make an offer and you might not be able to finance with certain types of loans since the interior isn't finished."

I said, "I want to make an offer. And financing won't be an issue. I already have it taken care of."

Paying for the house wouldn't be a problem. I was frugal with my money. Once Eve and I were married I insisted we keep our finances separate. I had no idea how much money she had in her savings—or if she even had any at all—and she didn't know I had enough money in my savings to buy a house and completely remodel it however *I* wanted. I preferred it that way.

Jim and I made our way back through the house. When we passed the room with the bag he said he'd insist a cleaning crew take care of it. I thought about pressing him again about what was in the bag but decided to wait.

Jim made sure all the lights were off and checked the lock on the back door. He locked the front door and put the key in a box attached to the knob.

Once we were to our vehicles he produced a folder full of papers. He went over everything in layman's terms. I knew I should read through them but I also knew what I was getting myself into. The house was as-is. Once I signed I couldn't bitch about anything wrong with the house because the bank that owned it wasn't obligated to fix anything. Whatever problems the structure had would be my responsibility.

I was about to sign the papers on the hood of Jim's vehicle but stopped with the pen a few centimeters from the dotted line.

I scrutinized Jim's expectant face and said, "What's in the bag?"

My question caught him off guard.

"Um, well," he sputtered. "A cleaning crew will take care of it. It'll be gone by the time you move in."

I sighed and set the pen down. "Isn't there a disclosure law? I'm not gonna sign anything until I know what's in the bag."

Jim avoided eye contact and said, "A dog."

His eyes dropped to his shoes. He nudged something on the ground with his toe and shoved his hands into his pockets. He looked like an embarrassed child caught doing something he knew was wrong. I found his actions amusing and expected him to throw himself on the ground in a tantrum at any moment.

I said, "A dog?"

He kept his eyes cast downward. "I think the previous tenant might've been disgruntled about losing their house. Sometimes homeowners will get the 'if I can't have it no one can attitude' and decide to trash the house before leaving. Some even destroy the furnace and water heaters and go as far as removing all the plumbing and electrical wiring to be spiteful." He finally made eye contact with me. "But the dog . . ." He shook his head. "It hadn't died naturally. I'm sorry, Mr. Graves, but it's a bit upsetting. Never in all the years have I encountered anything like it."

"Holy shit. Someone killed it? In the house?"

"You don't have anything to worry about. I assure you the locks have been replaced. I can even request for them to be replaced again before you move in."

I waved my hand dismissively. "I planned on installing a security system anyway."

He nodded. "You can never be too safe."

The mood turned sour and I wanted to put the thought of the dog out of my head. I also wanted Jim to forget about it. Having to relive the images made him uneasy and understandably so. I'm sure disposing of mutilated dog carcasses wasn't a regular requirement for a realtor. I picked up the pen with a flourish and signed the papers. Jim's stance eased when I made out a check for the earnest money. I handed him my business card which had my cell phone number, email, and office extension.

I said, "I'd prefer email when possible. You can call me at the office during business hours and leave a message if I'm out. Call my cell only if it's *absolutely* important. I want to keep this quiet."

He read my card and raised his eyebrows in surprise. He said, "An architect." He slipped the card into the folder along with the rest of my paperwork. "I guess that explains your fascination with the house."

I shook his sweaty hand again and we said our goodbyes. Once I was in my car I used copious amounts of hand sanitizer. I cleaned my hands three times but still felt filthy and swore I could still smell the stench of the dead dog. I checked my shoes to make sure I hadn't stepped in something rotten from the house before I started the car. I drove home with the windows down and grinned like an idiot when I fantasized about Eve's reaction to the house.

4

I kicked off my shoes in the hallway outside my apartment and picked them up. A strong odor of garlic and onions assaulted me once I was inside. Sounds of food preparation emanated from the kitchen.

"You're home," Eve called.

I sighed and dropped my keys on a table by the door. I was never sure why her greeting grated on my nerves. Because it wasn't really a greeting. It was a declaration of the obvious. I was home. I was aware I was home. She was aware I was home. She did not have to announce it to the world. Or better yet, announce it to the two people who already knew the information she was conveying.

I bit back my aggravation and replied, "Yeah."

I carried my shoes toward the hallway. Our washer and dryer were situated in a nook across from the bathroom. I opened the washer door, made sure the contents were not things needing transferred to the dryer, and threw my shoes in. Eve appeared in the kitchen doorway. I proceeded to strip off my clothes and add them to the load of laundry.

"I'm making Indian," she said. "I've been craving it all day. I can't believe how quick the pregnancy cravings hit." She sounded excited and vibrated with hyperactivity. "I've got my first doctor's appointment tomorrow."

She watched me expectantly. I continued to remove my

clothes. Her eyes flicked to my cock when I removed my underwear and she smiled. Her stance became more limber and she leaned against the doorframe.

Over the years I'd grown accustomed to Eve's subtle hints and mannerisms. It took me half a second to register her change in mood. She wanted sex. She didn't want sex at the moment. Having sex right then and there, hot and passionate, stinking and filthy, would be impulsive. Eve hadn't done anything sexually unpredictable in years. Even if she would've made a move I would've refused her. I was dirty. And over the last few years I wasn't in the mood when I felt dirty. It had been several years since the thought of fucking, or having an orgasm, was more enticing than being clean.

I fought the sudden urge to scream 'I don't want to fuck you'. And I sure as hell didn't want to fuck her later that night either. I wanted to tell her she was about to consume a massive amount of garlic and onions and those foods made her bloat up like a Dr. Seuss character and made her vagina smell weird and gross, not to mention she was a manipulative cunt and had ruined my life by getting knocked up on purpose, and fucking her for sexual pleasure was the furthest thing from my mind. I would hate fuck her with my fist at the drop of a hat if she wanted but that was about the extent of my affection at the moment.

Instead I said, "It smells like you're trying to kill a vampire."

Her smile wavered. She stood up straight and crossed her arms. She knew the remark was a passive aggressive one referring to the effects the food would have on her body. I told her early in our relationship her pussy could kill a vampire after she ate garlic. I knew it made her extremely self-conscious. But the gloves were off now. I agreed to pretend this marriage wasn't in shambles around family and friends. I never agreed to not be a prick when no one was around.

I turned and walked into the bathroom. "On site all day. Gonna take a shower." I shut the door.

"It'll be done in ten minutes," she called.

I took my time in the shower and fought the urge to masturbate when I soaped my penis. It had been a week and a half since Eve had acted interested in fucking. And I'd spent the last three nights researching houses and sending emails to realtors during my nightly alone time. I hadn't had time to jerk off. I was too busy constructing my revenge.

I didn't want to fuck Eve because I was mad at her. And if I fucked her I would have to take another shower to wash off the smelly vaginal juice and the sticky lube she preferred. If I came now I knew I wouldn't be able to get an erection later when *Eve* decided it was time to fuck. I smiled to myself. Not only would she not get what she wanted, but she always beat herself up whenever she wasn't able to arouse me. As if my lack of a sexual response was her fault and my attraction to her was slipping and there was nothing she could do to rectify it because no matter how hard she tried to get me hard my body wouldn't cooperate. My inability to get hard was never because of her appearance. It was mainly because I was getting old and tired and sometimes it was a chore to get aroused. But other times it was because the thought of getting dirty was unappealing and a mood killer.

I wanted my dick to be flaccid and inattentive to her. I started to masturbate, using water as lubricant. A sudden surge of anger flooded me as my cock grew hard. This was what she'd reduced me to—jerking off in the shower to spite her. I was doing this because she was selfish and I hated her for degrading me to this level of pettiness.

I grabbed Eve's conditioner, squeezed some onto the palm of my hand, and masturbated in an anger-induced frenzy. I came quickly. The orgasm was intense and I choked back a cry of pleasure. My stomach and leg muscles constricted and I put my hand on the wall to steady myself. I continued to stroke slowly as the semen ran down the shower wall. I cupped my hand and threw some water on it to rinse it down the drain. I thought, *That's exactly where the kid should be.* I re-washed my dick and hands and exited the shower.

Muffled clacking and clanging permeated the bathroom

walls as Eve set the table. I dried myself and retreated to our bedroom to dress. I pulled on a pair of black jeans and a gray cotton shirt and walked toward the kitchen.

Eve had begun without me and was halfway through her meal. A huge plate of steaming malai kofta sat on the table at my seat. The portion of food was almost double the amount I usually ate. A whole piece of naan slathered with olive oil and large chunks of garlic was situated on a plate to the side. I noticed Eve using a whole piece for herself. We normally shared one.

I sat and draped one of Eve's hideous floral patterned napkins across my lap. She was subtly hunched over her plate. She greedily ate her serving which, like mine, was double the normal portion. I lifted my naan and ripped it in half. I proceeded to scrape half of my food onto the plate with the naan. She stopped mid chew and stared at me dumbfounded. A dab of sauce clung to the corner of her mouth. I sat my plate in front of me gingerly and took a bite. She swallowed her food.

She said, "Something wrong?"

I shook my head and chewed. She eyed the third plate I'd created sitting between us and waited for me to explain. I couldn't take my eyes off the spot of sauce in the corner of her mouth.

"You gave me too much food," I said. "I'm not going to be one of those guys who gains thirty pounds because their wife got pregnant. Just because you want stretch marks doesn't mean I want my own set to match. I respect my body and like it the way it is."

She appeared crestfallen and peered down at her plate. She'd consumed three quarters of her meal. She sat her fork down and *finally* wiped the spot of sauce from her mouth with her napkin. My mouth contorted into a smirk. I continued to eat my supper.

With a neutral expression she said, "I have my first appointment tomorrow."

I responded by not replying and continued to eat as if she

hadn't spoken. I wanted to tell her she'd already informed me of the appointment and I didn't give a shit the first time she told me and still didn't give a shit. But I hated repeating myself and chose not to. She fingered her napkin nervously. I refused to show her any emotion beyond stoicism. I kept my expression apathetic and chewed my food. I had the absurd thought I must appear as emotionless as a cow chewing on grass.

"I want you to take me," she said.

"Why?"

She gave me an incredulous look and tilted her head. "Because you're the father?"

I shrugged. "Is it a requirement? Do they have to do a blood test or something?"

She laughed humorlessly. "We know who the father is."

"Do we?"

She stood, picked up her plate, and dumped the remaining food into the garbage disposal. She flipped the switch and rinsed her plate. I was getting tired of the temper tantrums involving running the garbage disposal. Once she was done she sat at the table again.

She clasped her hands together and placed them on the table. She composed herself and said, "Please go with me. Are you really going to make me take the bus?"

I never understood why she relied on public transit and other people to get around. It was annoying when she asked me to drive her considering I never wanted to do whatever it was she planned.

"Why do you want someone to go with you who doesn't want to be there, isn't happy about the situation, and will make *your* experience with all of it miserable?"

She thought about what I'd said with great deliberation but didn't respond.

I added, "I never said I'd go to the appointments or be your chauffeur. I never said I would play happy in front of a doctor. I'll pretend to be happy in front of friends and family. That's it."

"I don't want you to fake being happy. It's not part of the deal. I don't want you to be miserable."

"Too late."

She left the table. I finished my supper. The end of my meal was serenaded by the sounds of Eve's sobs emanating from our bedroom.

I cleaned my plate and headed to the study. Eve's crying quieted as I passed our bedroom. I imagined her lying on the bed and hearing my footsteps and waiting expectantly for me to enter and apologize for being an asshole and agree to go to her appointment and suddenly having a change of heart and becoming the happiest father in the world. Eve stifled another sob when I reached the study and I shut the door to block her out.

I turned on the computer and checked my email. I found a message from Jim Hagathorne and got excited. I knew I had to calm myself before opening it. My life had quickly become a shit heap over the past week. I had to prepare myself for disappointment. There was a possibility someone else already signed an agreement or was willing to pay a higher amount. The bank could reject my offer which was fifteen thousand dollars less than their asking price in the hopes I would give them more. I stared at the unopened email and thought, *This is a rejection.* I clicked on it, shut my eyes, and counted to ten to make sure the message was fully loaded before I read it.

It was an acceptance. I guffawed and clamped a hand over my mouth. I listened for Eve. It sounded as if she was finished with her crying jag. I waited a couple of beats with my hand over my mouth. I assumed Eve would compose herself and nosily come to check why her husband was laughing. She remained in the bedroom and I sadistically hoped she thought I was laughing at her. I dropped my hand and reread the message.

The message contained a list of documents he needed scanned and emailed to his office. Luckily most of what he wanted was located in a filing cabinet I kept in the study. Some of the items I was able to retrieve online. There was also an attachment of a PDF I needed to print, sign, scan, and send back. The process kept me busy for the next hour.

When I was almost done another email arrived from Mr. Crutch. His message stated he'd had a conversation with Sam about my situation. He also wrote he would be in the office tomorrow afternoon. He requested I stop in and not to worry about the meeting. From the content of the email I assumed I was set to work from home. I had a brief moment of panic and thought he could possibly tell me I couldn't work from home. What would I do with the house if this was the case? It was too far away to commute back and forth. I would have to withdraw the offer. I thought, *Maybe it would be better to wait until after the meeting before sending the realtor all the paperwork he needed.* It would be less of a waste of time on both fronts if I didn't end up working from home.

I ran my hands through my hair, leaned back in the chair, and took a few deep breaths. *Fuck it.* I could always freelance or start my own business. I had enough money in the bank to cover the cost of the house and the repairs and updates *and* I would still have a sizable amount to live off for a while. We would need money for utilities and the car payment. I could get a job with a local contractor. I was a little on the old side but physically fit. I reread Mr. Crutch's message and was positive from the wording he was going to allow me to work from home.

I let the acceptance from the bank and the positive tone of Mr. Crutch's email nurture what small amount of happiness I still harbored in my heart. I knew this could all crash down somehow or another but I was going to ride the wave of excitement as much as possible until it happened. I responded to Mr. Crutch's email to confirm I would be there. I put the worries out of my head—especially the ones about not being able to work from home—and gathered the last of the information for the realtor. When I finished sending everything over to Jim I realized I was humming.

I exited the study and decided to watch an hour or two of television before going to bed. Normally I would read but I was too excited to keep my head in a book. Eve hated my obsession with documentaries but she filled the time I took over the television with grading papers or reviewing lesson plans. She was more apt to watch whatever mainstream nighttime drama the major networks aired. She never said anything if I wanted to watch something during her shows because she recorded everything on the DVR.

Our bedroom door was shut and the apartment was quiet. I entered the living room and turned the television on. I wondered if Eve was so pissed she'd left. I spotted her filthy shoes by the door. It appeared she'd chosen to go to bed early. Good. Having her in the same room right now would ruin how happy I was about the house approval.

I tried to focus on the television but my mind wandered to the house and what materials I wanted to use for remodeling. I hadn't thought about how much what I was doing would piss off Eve. My head was filled with possibilities and how nice it would be to stay in a house you designed and be able to enjoy the art of what you'd chosen for the structure. I decided a celebration was in order.

We always kept a couple bottles of liquor in the kitchen in case someone stopped by. And sometimes one of us would have a particularly heinous day and would have a drink to take the edge off. Neither one of us were everyday drinkers.

I made my way to the kitchen and poured a generous amount of whiskey into a glass. I sipped some over the sink before proceeding back into the living room. I nursed the drink for a couple hours and watched a documentary about abandoned locations across the world. The alcohol did what it was designed to do. I was relaxed and warm and became engrossed in the haunted appearance of a ghost town in one segment of the documentary. When the show was over I decided to turn in.

I shut the television off and took my glass to the kitchen. It wasn't until I stood that I realized how inebriated I was. It had been a while since I'd had a drink and the amount I poured was more than my usual. I deposited the glass in the sink and made my way to the bathroom.

I pissed, washed my hands, and stared at my reflection. The mirror showed a grinning fool. The alcohol made me feel good and I was happy about the house and the probability of working from home. There wasn't much more I could ask for other than something happening to the stupid kid growing in Eve's belly. I hoped she would have a miscarriage so I could divorce her immediately after, before she could wrap her head around what had happened. Because it wasn't until tonight I realized I would only be happy if I did the things I wanted, and got the things I wanted, and all of it was exactly *how* I wanted. And the only way to obtain those things was if I was alone. I was aware I was a miserable and selfish motherfucker and was fine with it.

I shut the lights off throughout the apartment and stumbled into our dark bedroom. The darkness made the drunkenness disorienting. I tried to undress quietly and not wake Eve or trip over something. I slipped into bed in my underwear and lay on my back with my eyes shut and embraced the sensation of spinning and twisting and falling produced by the alcohol. I was content. And I felt justified about what I was doing, and how I was doing it, because it was all for me and fuck anyone who didn't like it.

Eve rolled over. She laid her hand on my chest and stroked it. She was awake. This was her unimaginative way of instigating sex. I wanted to push her hand away and roll over because I was mad. I'd planned on denying her. But she fingered my hair softly and kissed my shoulder. She slid her hand down to my dick and I was surprised at my body's response. I was hard. It was a combination of the alcohol and my excitement over the house that put me in the mood to fuck.

I let Eve stroke my cock through the material of my underwear. She eventually slid her hand into my underwear and stroked my hard on. I made no movement to pleasure her. I figured this was equal to not fucking her. She kissed me on the mouth and recoiled.

"You've been drinking," she whispered.

"Mmm."

She paused briefly and tugged my underwear to convey she wanted me to remove them. I did what she wanted clumsily and lay on my back again. There was a rustling beside me as she undressed. I chased off the thought of lube and smelly vaginal juices and focused on fucking and getting off and doing this to spite her in some form or another. Her hands groped at my chest and she repositioned on the bed and kissed my stomach before taking my dick into her mouth. I moaned involuntarily as she worked. Oral sex had become nearly obsolete over the years unless she wanted something from me. I couldn't bring myself to eat her cunt anymore without gagging.

I let her do all the work and at some point I laid my hand on the back of her head. She pulled her mouth off my penis and batted my hand away. Eve hated it when I held her head during oral. I waited until she began sucking me again and placed my hand on the back of her head and forced my dick into her mouth. She gagged and pulled away from me.

"God damn it, Nick! Stop!"

I sat up and fought the vertigo of alcohol. I found her in the dark sitting on her haunches. I grabbed her arm and forced her onto her hands and knees. She made some irritated sounds. I worked up some saliva as I positioned myself behind her ass. I spat on my hand, thought about how disgusted I was going to feel in the morning, and slathered the secretion on my cock. I quickly thrust all of my manhood into Eve's vagina. She gasped at the unexpected full intrusion. I grabbed her hips and began pounding as hard and quick as I could. I hate fucked her. I hate fucked her with everything my drunken body could produce and she made small sounds of protest and impatience. I struggled to keep from falling over as I drunkenly jackhammered her. The bed's rocking rhythm fought against mine. I focused on getting off and not on the sweat forming on my body and the slime of her vagina contaminating me. She huffed and I thought about how she betrayed me and how the baby of that betrayal was growing in her stomach. I could feel the orgasm building. I fucked her and knew we were both going to have bruises because of the ferocity. And I did something I hadn't done in a long time. I spanked Eve's ass. I spanked her hard. I hit her ass harder than I'd ever done at the beginning of our relationship when sex was animalistic and out of control. She cried out. It wasn't a cry of pleasure though. It was a cry of pain. The knowledge of her pain sent me over the edge and I came. Once all of my seed was spilled I collapsed beside her. Eve slipped out of bed before it stopped moving and headed toward the bathroom without a word.

I passed out shortly after she disappeared and without cleaning the sex off my cock or putting my underwear on. I dreamed our apartment was abandoned and I was a disembodied soul who patiently sat in the living room for decades. Time slowly passed and the paint on the walls darkened with mold. The carpet rotted and weeds snaked their way through the floorboards and climbed the walls. Years of dust collected on Eve's furniture. And right before I woke the walls began to crumble and collapse around me.

I woke to my alarm for work. I was spread out haphazardly on the bed and alone. I was covered in the dry and foul secretions of sex. I shamefully rolled out of bed and headed directly for the shower.

5

Mr. Crutch's office door was open. He was in the middle of a phone conversation. I stood in the doorway and waited for him to acknowledge me. His chair was turned and he faced the window as he talked. I raised my hand to rap on the doorframe but decided to wait until he noticed me.

I ran my hand over my hair nervously to smooth it down. I knew there wasn't a hair out of place but I always had the feeling Mr. Crutch didn't care for its length. Whenever we talked his eyes wandered over it. I wasn't sure if it was because he was close to seventy and his hair was gray and balding and he envied mine or if he despised it because I wasn't clean-cut.

The term clean-cut always bothered me. People used it to describe a shaven man with close cropped hair. I imagined Mr. Crutch used the phrase to describe the haircut he wanted when he visited his barber. I couldn't envision him at a high end salon similar to the one I visited. No. He would go to a barber. He visited an old man like himself who complained about kids these days and their girlish hair and they would talk about other old men who'd died since the last time they'd seen each other. I imagined he used Pert shampoo and a dab of Brylcreem to sculpt it into the perfect and unchanging style he'd worn since he was a teenager. His office always had a medicinal smell I associated with cheap soap.

I personally didn't find anything about Mr. Crutch clean beyond his suit. His skin was thin and covered in age spots so thick his face appeared dirty and coffee stained. His nose was bulbous and pitted and lined with broken blood vessels. And his fingernails had a yellow tinge and were always in dire need of trimming.

I inspected my own short nails. Mr. Clutch turned his chair and glanced at me. He motioned for me to take a seat.

Before I made it to the chair he covered the mouth piece of his phone and said, "Close the door," and continued his conversation with the person on the line.

I sat and pretended to be interested in the family photos he displayed on his desk. In the photos his wife appeared older than he. I wondered if I was looking at a photo of him and his mother. The woman had a thin halo of white curly hair and a slight hunchback. Mr. Crutch explained the schematics of a certain structure to the person on the phone. I tried to imagine what Eve would look like when she was seventy. Would she end up with a hunchback and saggy tits like Mrs. Crutch? It seemed inevitable. We were all falling apart a little every day. But I was intentionally trying to preserve myself as much as possible. I thought Eve was into preserving her body also until she intentionally got pregnant. Now I didn't know anymore. She was bound to get fat and grow stretch marks and her tits would swell and get veiny and even if she did lose the weight afterward her whole body was going to sag. Then would come the wrinkles and the age spots in a couple of years and god knew what else. Eve's mother was fat and in the back of my mind I knew Eve would never bother to lose the weight after having the kid. She would see it as her badge of accomplishment for shitting out a kid. I hated it when a frumpy woman explained away her weight and appearance and lack of style with the number of children she'd given birth to. It was a weak excuse for letting yourself go, giving up, and not giving a shit if your loved ones were embarrassed of you.

Mr. Crutch hung up the phone. He noticed me checking

out the photos and smiled.

"So," he said. "Sam tells me you want to work from home."

"Yes, sir."

"Says ya got a baby on the way."

"Yes, sir."

"When's she due?"

My first thought was he didn't know Eve's name. I wasn't offended though. I didn't know his wife's name. We were even. I had a moment of panic when realizing I had no idea when Eve was having the kid. How much longer did I have free of shit and vomit and piss and crying?

He smirked and shook his head. His crooked smile deepened all the wrinkles on his face. "You don't have a clue, do you?"

"Uh, well . . ." I fumbled. "She's got an appointment today."

"Don't worry." He waved his hand dismissively. "Marriage, babies, kids . . . all that stuff's what women get excited about. It's best to stay out of their way and let them do whatever they want. They'll do it anyway and make your life hell in the process."

I gave him a chagrined smile.

He leaned back in his chair and said, "About the working from home business . . . I'm not going to lie. When Sam mentioned you were willing to take a pay cut my ears perked up."

I nodded and prepared myself. I could lose a substantial amount of my salary. But the loss would be worth what I would gain in the end.

He laced his fingers together and laid his hands in his lap. "I'm a business man. It's my job to get the best deal for my money. But I'm not a heartless bastard. You've got a child on the way. You're going to need all the funds you can get."

I nodded. "Yes, sir."

"Tell me why you'd want to work from home. Sam says yer gonna be a stay-at-home dad?"

Here was my chance to convince him this was a good

idea. "Well, sir. As you know," I waved my hand toward a photo of his grandchildren, "a child brings a lot of change. The apartment we live in has two bedrooms but it's small. I found the perfect house for our expanding family but it's two hours away."

I leaned forward in my chair. "I like my job here, Mr. Crutch. I've got seniority. And I can't complain about my salary. I want to continue working for you, but . . . I'm really in love with this structure." I flinched at the coldness of the word 'structure'. "I mean house."

He said, "This is why I like ya. You've got a real passion for architecture." He paused. "What's your wife gonna do? She's a professor, right? Are there any colleges near the home?"

"She's an elementary teacher," I said. "And, uh, no . . . actually, there aren't any schools in the area. We plan on homeschooling."

"So you'll both be stay-at-home parents?"

"Yes, sir."

He nodded and pursed his lips. "Very modern I suppose."

I didn't know if I should take his statement as a bad sign. Would he tell me no if he knew Eve would be at home full-time also? Mr. Crutch was probably old fashioned. The kind of man who thought a woman's place was in the home and the man was the bread winner who went to work every day.

"I'm not going to let you sweat this," he said. "I don't see any reason why you can't work from home for the same salary . . . as long as all of your work is completed, and I don't get any complaints from the clients, and you're able to come in for meetings."

"The work will be done. You won't hear any complaints. And you can call me anytime and I'll be here in two hours."

"Well then." He stood up and extended his hand for me to shake. "You'll have to talk with Sam and let him know when you want to start."

I stood and shook his hand. "Thank you, sir. I promise I won't let you down."

"Congratulations on the baby. I hope he, or she, is healthy. You're gonna love being a father."

I tried not to grimace and said, "Thank you. I'm sure I will."

6

I could smell steak and potatoes when I entered the apartment. Eve didn't make her usual announcement I was home. This meant she was mad. Normally I would be on high alert because I knew there would be an argument later but I didn't care. There wasn't anything she could say to bring down my level of enthusiasm. Her remarks would only annoy me.

I dropped my shoes in the washer and thought about how everything was clicking into place. I informed Sam as soon as I knew when I was moving and wanted a week of vacation time to get everything settled in our new place. After the week vacation I would begin working from home. Jim Hagathorne responded by email to let me know all my information had been passed on to the appropriate people and since I was not financing the house the closing would most likely be in a couple of weeks. I only had a few other things to square away before moving out of the city and would take care of those between tonight and tomorrow.

Eve was in the kitchen eating dinner. There was only one plate of food prepared and it sat in front of her. She slowly cut her steak and didn't acknowledge me. There were no pots or pans on the stovetop containing food. I opened the oven door and found it empty also. I proceeded to the fridge and didn't find anything extra from the meal Eve was consuming. I did however find the leftover Indian food and proceeded to reheat it.

By the time I sat at the table she was almost done with her food. I gave her an apathetic expression and began to eat. She finally made eye contact and gave me such a sour expression I would have thought the last few bites of her food had gone bad.

I knew she wanted me to ask about the appointment. But I wasn't going to. The only thing I did want to know was when the unwanted inconvenience would arrive screaming into this world to ruin my life. But there was no way I would give Eve the slightest amount of satisfaction by admitting any interest in the kid.

She finished her plate and did the dishes. When she was done she headed toward the living room but stopped in the doorway.

She turned to me and said coldly, "I put the air mattress in the study for you."

She didn't wait for me to reply. She disappeared into the living room and the television began its drone of the designated lowest common denominator programming.

This was her way of being a bitch. She didn't get mad and yell or throw things. She did things without explaining herself and made snarky passive-aggressive remarks and walked away. It could be worse. Her methods might work on some other poor sap. But I was too stubborn. When she was mad the apartment was quiet except for the television. I rather liked it.

Sleeping in the study didn't bother me either. I don't know why she thought it did. Besides, I needed to get hold of some contractors and would spend most of the night in there anyway. Just to be spiteful I extended both arms in the direction where I thought she might be sitting on the sofa and lifted both of my middle fingers. I waved my arms around in a dance and mouthed the word 'cunt'. I knew the gesture was childish but it made me feel better.

I finished my dinner, washed my plate, and proceeded to

the study. The twin air mattress lay in the corner. A haphazard pile of blankets and pillows was thrown on it.

I sat at my computer and sent emails to a few contractors I knew. I let them know about the tight timeline, making sure to apologize for the poor advance notice. When I finished I researched local urologists.

Dr. Russell's office was located two blocks from work. The online review sites stated he was one of the best in the area. He also had a form on his website to set up an appointment which was a plus. I disliked using the phone and the more things I could do online the better. I completed the form and submitted it.

I checked the clock. It was late. The apartment was quiet. I didn't hear the television and had been so engrossed in what I was doing I hadn't noticed when Eve shut it off. She would be in bed by this time. I opened the door and found the apartment dark. I crept into the kitchen and poured some whiskey into a glass and returned to the study. Dr. Russell's office had already replied to my submission with an appointment for the next day. I assumed his appointment scheduling must be automated by a computer when no one was in the office. There was a link in the email if I needed to cancel the appointment or reschedule. I wrote down the information, along with all the instructions of things to wear and bring, and deleted the email.

I sipped the whiskey and began to scour the internet for porn. Another email arrived in my inbox. It was from one of the contractors. It stated his crew would be able to take the remodeling job and have it completed within a week. I replied with a short message that I'd call him tomorrow with more information.

I continued to search for porn. I stumbled across an S&M video of a blonde girl who barely looked eighteen. Normally I would have passed but there was something about the girl that reminded me of Eve. I clicked the play button and slid the time bar past the first ten minutes.

The video buffered and began to play. The girl's hair was

disheveled and her hands were tied behind her back. She wore a dog collar and there were streaks of black mascara running down her cheeks from crying. She was on her knees and two men stood beside her. The shot only showed the men from the waist down, their cocks were angled in strange directions, and both of them stroked themselves slowly.

One man bent down and attached clamps to the girl's nipples. She whimpered and another tear slid down her cheek.

I took a drink of the whiskey and unfastened my pants.

The other man grabbed a handful of the girl's hair and inserted his dick into her mouth. The girl gagged. For the next few minutes the guy fucked her in the mouth and she gagged and cried.

I stroked my cock and focused on the girl's face. I tried to replace the girl's face with Eve's.

The man who'd clamped the girl's nipples was positioning himself behind her now. He got down on his knees and the man in front of the girl withdrew his penis from her mouth and let go of her hair. The man behind the girl grabbed her dog collar forcefully and pushed her forward. She probably would have fallen on her face if he hadn't held the collar. The girl's face was red and strained from the collar strangling her. She tried to move her tied hands behind her back. The man behind her spit on her asshole and rammed his cock in her ass. She let out a garbled cry.

I closed my eyes and thought of fucking Eve in the ass in the same manner. I wanted her to bawl and cry out in pain. I masturbated.

The girl in the video began to cough. I opened my eyes. The man was butt fucking her with such force I expected both of them to fall down. He held the collar tight and was red faced and sweating. I focused on the girl's pained face and continued to jerk off.

The other man grabbed a handful of the girl's hair and lifted her head. The guy behind her let go of the collar and grabbed her hips to steady himself as he continued to fuck her. The man gripping the girl's hair stuck his cock in her mouth before she had a chance to take a full breath.

Both men fucked the young girl as if she were merely an object instead of a human being. I was getting off on her level of discomfort more than the fucking. I jerked off and focused on her tortured face. The orgasm came quick and I almost didn't grab a tissue in time to catch my come. I left my pants undone with my penis exposed and watched the video for a few more minutes. I finished the rest of the whiskey and closed the window before the two men decided to jerk off on the girl's face. I fastened my pants and walked to the restroom. I flushed the spent tissue and washed my hands.

I returned to the study and set an alarm on my cellphone, turned off the light, and lay down on the air mattress. I tried not to think about my appointment tomorrow and drifted to sleep feeling good about the direction my life was headed.

7

I arrived at Dr. Russell's office fifteen minutes before my appointment. I was impressed with the waiting room. The walls and furniture were done in soft whites. Even the floors were a whitewashed hard wood. A large saltwater aquarium was located beside the receptionist's window. The waiting room design was more for an upscale spa but I found it comforting. The only thing missing was the New Age music.

The receptionist was an attractive middle-aged woman. Her hair was shoulder length and brown with scant wisps of gray to let you know it was her natural color. She had a few wrinkles around her eyes and mouth. She was the type of woman a man wished his wife would transition into when she reached that age. She scanned my insurance information, handed me some paperwork to fill out, and asked me to have a seat.

I was the only patient in the waiting area. I took steady breaths and ignored the nervousness growing in the pit of my stomach. I signed the paperwork and returned it to the receptionist. She assured me a nurse would come for me shortly. I grabbed a magazine from one of the various tables littered with things to fill a patient's wait and took a seat. I flipped through the pages without reading. My mind was preoccupied with what was about to happen.

"Mr. Graves?"

A pretty brunette woman in black scrubs stood in a doorway leading to the exam rooms. She cradled a clipboard in the crook of her arm.

I stood and set the magazine on the nearest table. My hands were slightly damp with nervousness. I wiped them on the sides of my jeans as I approached the nurse. She smiled at me.

She said, "My name's Greta. I'm gonna be your nurse. Let's head back this way and get your weight." She turned and motioned for me to follow her.

She had a bounce in her step I could only associate with the young who hadn't been trampled on by life. I stared at her tight, perfect ass as she swiftly walked down the hall. Normally I would be aroused by Greta's firm body but all I could think about was large needles and scalpels sharpening themselves for my testicles. My penis retracted instead.

Greta led me to a nook containing a scale and a chair designed for drawing blood. She asked me to stand on the scale. I did as I was told. The scale had a small digital screen mounted on the wall. The numbers flashed once the device settled and Greta wrote my weight on a paper attached to the clipboard.

She asked, "How ya doin' so far?"

"Nervous," I said. I wiped my sweaty palms on my pants again.

Greta made a sympathetic sound. I half expected her to follow it with a 'you poor baby' and a comforting pat on the arm.

She said, "It's normal to be nervous. Don't worry. You're in good hands with Dr. Russell. It'll be over with before you know it." She smiled. "Are you ready to head back to the exam room?"

Exam room? I thought. *You mean torture room.* I nodded and let her guide me to a small room with the standard equipment: an exam table, a sink, a few plain cabinets, a regular chair, a stool on wheels, and a stainless steel table with wheels. There was also a computer monitor and keyboard. The screen displayed an outdated screensaver of pipes constructing themselves out of thin air in various colors. I always hated that screensaver.

Greta instructed me to sit in the chair and took my blood pressure and temperature. Once she was done she woke the computer, entered a complicated password, and proceeded to enter all the health information she had collected from me. She provided me with a paper gown and told me to strip off my pants and underwear and put on the gown so it opened in front. She promised to return in a few minutes and left me to partially disrobe.

I followed her directions and sat on the exam table. The table was cold on my ass through the paper gown. The crinkling of the gown did nothing to soothe my nerves. I closed my eyes and tried to think of anything else to relax. There was a knock at the door. I opened my eyes. The door opened a few inches.

"Mr. Graves? Are you dressed for me to come in?" Greta said.

"Yes."

She reentered with a plastic container full of liquid and a disposable razor. She sat the items on the counter. She retrieved and pulled on a pair of latex gloves.

Greta said, "I'm going to shave and disinfect the surgery area."

"Dear god," I groaned.

Greta giggled. "It's okay, Mr. Graves. This is part of my job. I do it all the time. Believe me . . . if you've seen one scrotum you've seen them all. Now," she laid a hand on my shoulder, "if you'd just lay back on the table I'll be done in a jiffy."

I reluctantly lay on my back and she opened my gown. She popped the yellow protective plastic piece off the razor and dropped it in the trash can. She whisked the razor in the container full of liquid and bubbles formed on the surface. I shut my eyes.

"This is humiliating," I said.

"Try to relax," she said. "You're going to feel me touch you."

The tacky latex of her gloves touched my balls and she pulled the skin taunt.

"I'm going to begin shaving," she said. "Please lay still."

I was a statue. There were few things in this world more terrifying than having a razor held to your testicles. If she didn't want me to move I would become cement. I decided to hold my breath also in case it caused my balls to move in the slightest while she worked.

I kept my eyes shut. Warm water dripped down my scrotum and pooled into the crack of my ass. Greta pulled the razor over my balls and whisked it in the water after every stroke. I felt her exhalations against my wet skin as she worked. I took breaths whenever she was cleaning the razor in the water and held it while she worked. My penis retracted farther than I ever thought possible although under different circumstances I might have found this hot woman shaving me erotic.

"All done," she chimed. "I'm going to dry you and swab the area with iodine."

There was no way I was ever going to be able to look this woman in the face again. The whole scenario was dirty and more like going to a whore house than a doctor's office. I continued to keep my eyes shut as she patted my groin and ass crack with paper towels. She wiped my balls with something cold. Before I knew it she announced she was done. Water began to run in the sink and I reluctantly opened my eyes.

Greta dumped the shaving water down the drain. She threw the container holding the water in the garbage, deposited the razor in the sharps bin on the wall, and snapped her gloves into the trash. She pulled on a fresh pair of gloves and wheeled a small steel table from the wall over beside me. She opened a drawer and produced a paper cover for the table and several different sterilized packages. Greta popped open the packages quickly and laid two scary scissor utensils on the table along with a small vile of clear liquid, a hypodermic needle, a bandage, a piece of papery material, and what appeared to be thread and a curved needle.

I stared at the curved needle and fear curled into a tight ball in my gut and made my spine tingle. A thin layer of cold sweat instantly formed over my body and my scalp crawled. I took a deep breath and the chemical smell of disinfects burned my throat. My stomach churned in such a way that I wasn't sure if I needed to vomit or pass gas.

"You can sit up if you want," she said. "Dr. Russell will be right in."

She was out of the exam room before I could sit up all the way. I calmed myself and looked down at my naked balls. They felt cold and exposed. I felt violated. I closed the paper gown.

Someone knocked on the door and opened it. The doctor entered. I expected an old man in a white lab coat. Instead a man who looked ten years younger than me entered in black scrubs. He hooked his fingers under the seat of the squat stool and hurriedly wheeled it toward me and extended his hand at the same time. We shook hands and he positioned the stool directly in front of me without sitting on it.

"Dr. Russell," he said.

He proceeded to the sink and scrubbed his hands. The residual touch of his handshake bothered me. I knew doctors were required to wash hands between patients but this doctor touched men's penises all day. I wiped my hand on the paper gown and watched him wash his hands thoroughly. When he was finished he pulled on a pair of latex gloves and sat on the stool. His head was at crotch level. He laced his gloved fingers together and held his hands away from his body, resting his elbows on his knees.

He said, "Do you have any questions about the vasectomy before I start?"

"Can you knock me out for it?"

He smirked. "You can keep your eyes closed if you don't

want to watch. You'll feel a pinch from the needle when I numb the area but after you won't feel any pain. I'm sorry I can't give you anything else. Are you ready or would you like to wait a few more minutes?"

"I'm as ready as I'm gonna get."

He used his upper arms to grip the steel table of instruments and wheeled it into position by his side, careful not to touch anything with his gloved hands. He filled the hypodermic needle from the vile and set it back on the table. The germaphobe inside me relaxed but the part of me about to have this procedure was on edge. It was difficult to take my eyes off the needle. The doctor opened my robe. He picked up the papery material from the cart, unfolded it, and placed it under my balls.

"I'm going to find your vas deferens," he said.

Dr. Russell leaned forward and fondled my balls with his left hand, stretching the skin with his thumb and forefinger. Once he was satisfied with what he'd found he picked up the needle with his right hand. I closed my eyes and grabbed the table like I was holding on for my life.

"Okay," Dr. Russell said. "I'm going to administer the numbing agent. You're going to feel a pinch. Are you ready?"

"Yes."

"I want you to take a deep breath and hold it."

I did what he told me. He counted to three and the needle pierced the skin. It was not pleasant. I wanted to punch Dr. Russell in the face. But it wasn't the most painful thing to happen to my balls either. Once in high school I got into a fight with a classmate and he kneed me in the balls so hard I vomited. This was bad. But it wasn't that bad. And within a few seconds the pain was gone.

"The worst part is over," he said.

I kept my eyes closed and listened to him move things around on the table. I couldn't feel his hands on my balls anymore. The sweat on my body began to dry and I felt chilly.

"Do you want me to tell you what I'm doing as I do it?" he asked.

"I want you to tell me when it's over."

He picked something off the table.

"Did you have this done?" I asked.

"Yes. I have three kids. The wife and I thought three was enough." He paused. "How many kids do you have?"

"One too many."

A tugging sensation in the pit of my stomach caused me to open my eyes but I didn't look down. I took a deep breath and shut my eyes again. He continued without another word. The room's silence was broken occasionally with the clack of instruments on the metal table.

Eventually the paper under my balls crinkled and he said, "All right. All done."

I opened my eyes as he gently applied a bandage to my balls. He used his forearms again to move the table with the instruments away. He removed the papery material from behind my balls and discarded it in the trash along with his gloves.

He proceeded to wash his hands and run down a checklist, "We'll give you a script for some pain medication. Take it if you need it. Put some ice on it when you get home and take it easy over the weekend. Don't do anything strenuous and don't forget to wear snug underwear. It will help with the pulling sensation." He turned the water off, pulled towels from a dispenser, and dried his hands. "You can remove the bandage tomorrow and shower. I'd suggest letting the bandage soak in the shower for a few minutes to soften the adhesive before you try to remove it. We'll send you a reminder in three months to come back for a check up to make sure your sperm count is zero. Greta will give you a paper with all this info. If you have any major discomfort don't be afraid to call." He tossed the towels he'd been drying his hands on in the trash. "Questions?"

I shook my head. He extended his hand and I shook it. I wasn't as bothered by his handshake this time because it was my own penis he'd been handling. But the fact he tortured penises for a living and didn't seem to be bothered by it was disconcerting nonetheless.

"Take it easy," he said and left the room without ceremony.

I dressed with care and gingerly made my way toward the waiting room. Greta met me at the receptionist's desk. She gave me the list of care instructions along with a prescription for pain medication. I left the office with short slow steps.

Once I was outside I made my way to the car with a bowlegged step I invented to assure my balls were not being abused since I couldn't feel them. I felt like a cowboy making his way down Main Street for a high noon shoot out. Once I was behind the wheel of my car I thought, *I'm pretty good at making major life decisions.*

8

I spent most of the weekend secluded in the study. Eve and I ignored one another whenever we were in the same room. We drifted through the apartment like two disembodied spirits, unaware of the other.

Occasionally I would make a trip to the kitchen for food. She never offered me any of the food she prepared and only made enough for herself. Mostly I only left the study to obtain more ice for my sore balls. She didn't seem to care or be aware of my overconsumption of ice.

Eve left Saturday afternoon without telling me where she was going or when she would be back. Not that I cared. I didn't give a shit. But letting the other person know where you were and about what time you would be home had always been a courtesy we'd both exercised in case there was an emergency. I wasn't a jealous person or one of those guys who grills their partner about who they've been hanging out with.

Actually, I would be happy if she was screwing someone. It would give me a good excuse to tell her to go fuck herself and move into the house without the overwhelming sense of doom she oozed whenever she was near. Lately whenever she wasn't around there was an all-consuming sensation of relief. The silence of the apartment made me content and I let the peacefulness of solitude saturate my soul whenever I had a few seconds of bliss to myself. It was freeing and invigorating. It was exhausting when your home life was the equivalent of walking blindfolded through a maze of landmines. I knew one wrong step was going to leave me in the middle of an argument I had no intention of being in . . . or with my leg blown off. At this point phantom limb syndrome was preferable.

Shortly after Eve left I refilled my cup with ice. I returned to the study and nestled the cup between my legs. I called the contractor. We conversed about the specific materials I wanted for the house and the quantity needed. He asked if there was anything specific Eve would like done.

"It's all kinda hush hush," I said.

My cell phone was on speaker and I set it on the desk. The screen displayed a counter with the amount of time I'd been on the phone with Alan. Some rustling emanated from the phone's tiny speakers and the sound became distorted.

"Okay," he said. "Here it is. Twelve by twelve black slate tile. Let's see . . . for the square footage you gave me you're looking at a total of—"

"Alan, I'm not interested in the cost. I know how much it'll cost. I want you to tell me you'll have the materials on hand to finish the project within a week. If you don't have everything, or you don't have an experienced worker, I want to know. I'll hire a second contractor who has the supplies, or experience, to do a job while you work on something else."

I shifted in the chair, mindful of my bruised scrotum, and readjusted the cup of melting ice. I listened for any sign Eve had come home. Soft clicking sounds came from the phone and Alan sighed. I imagined him typing to check his inventory.

"I don't mean to be a dick," I said, "but there's no loyalty on this. I don't care about the cost. It's who can finish the job the quickest with the correct materials and have it look perfect. I know it's a lot to ask but you'll be compensated for your hard work."

"You don't have to make excuses. I knew what I was getting into when I signed up." There was a brief pause. "It looks like we definitely have everything on hand. But I'm going to double check. I'll go over to storage tomorrow and make sure there's no damage. Sometimes the kids I hire damage things when unloading the trucks . . . like a tile, and they just ignore it. Then inventory is screwed and we have four tiles less than what's in the computer. Kids are assholes, man. You know how they are . . . they don't give a shit about anything unless it's theirs and they want it."

"Wouldn't know. Don't have any kids." *For now*, I thought.

"Lucky you," he mumbled. "Bunch of ungrateful bastards."

There was an awkward pause. I checked the phone to make sure we hadn't been disconnected. The screen flashed to signal an incoming call and beeped.

"Hey, Alan, I hate to rush off but I'm getting a call from the realtor."

He sounded distracted. "Oh, okay. I'll call you tomorrow about the inventory."

"Thanks. Appreciate it. Later."

I reached forward and touched the phone to switch to the incoming call before Alan could respond. An ache raced through my groin when I shifted. I sat back slowly.

"Hello?" I half groaned.

"Nick? Jim Hagathorne." He breathed heavily.

"Hey, Jim."

"I have good news and weird news."

"Not bad news?"

"I wouldn't call it bad news just . . . weird." He laughed nervously. "The bank called today and they're ready to close on Friday."

"They called on a Saturday? Weird."

"I know. That's what I thought too. But that's not the weird part." His mouth breathing sounded wet. "I guess they *really* want to get out from under the house. And that's where the weird part comes in. I wouldn't feel right if I didn't tell you."

"Don't tell me the house was built on an ancient Indian burial ground."

Jim gave a forced laugh. "Not quite. But it does have to do with the mess we found." He paused. The only sound was his breathing. "The bank sent in the cleaning crew and they found some more . . . stuff."

"What kinda *stuff*?"

"I guess what I bagged wasn't all of it."

"There wasn't anything else. We were all over the place. We would've noticed something."

"That's what I told them. The lady I spoke to was very accusatory . . . like they thought we were responsible."

"What?" I barked.

"I know. I know. I was angry too." He coughed and cleared his throat. "My reputation as a realtor is very important. I can't have a bank start a rumor like this. I could lose my job."

"Was it another dog?"

"Uh, no. They found some . . . sculptures."

"What kind of sculptures?"

"Mr. Graves—"

"Nick. Please call me Nick."

"Nick. I don't know how to say this without sounding vulgar."

I laughed and instantly regretted it. It felt like someone was flicking my nuts with each contraction of my stomach muscles. I cleared my throat to cover my discomfort.

I said, "Believe me, I've heard it all. If you work with enough contractors, and visit enough construction sites, you'll learn things you wish you hadn't."

There was a moment of hesitancy on his end. "They found two life-sized, anatomically correct sculptures of a man and a woman. There was evidence someone may have recently had intercourse with them."

"What the fuck?" I whispered.

"The sculptures were made out of . . ." There was long

pause. He mumbled something unintelligible.

"I didn't catch what you said."

"Feces."

I stared at the phone, not sure if I'd heard him correctly.

"Shit," I said. "They were made out of shit."

"Yes."

I blinked rapidly. "Someone was having sex with shit dolls in the house." I said it more as an affirmation and not a question. I couldn't believe what I heard.

"Yes. I felt you needed to know. I wouldn't feel comfortable not telling you." Jim's voice sounded faint as I processed what he said. "Full disclosure only applies if the buyer asks for information. I'm not required to tell you unless you ask. If you're still planning to purchase this property I think you should have a security system installed. The bank filed a report and the local police have taken the sculptures as evidence. There's an ongoing investigation. The police are sure it was teenagers playing a prank and nothing else will happen once the residence is occupied."

"Uh huh. Sounds like a pretty elaborate prank for teenagers."

"My thoughts exactly. Personally, if I were you, I would cancel the agreement and look for another house. I know you're starting a family. I don't feel right about selling a house to someone with little ones when there might be a lunatic trying to break in. It sounds like the previous owner may be insane."

"*May be* insane?"

"I'm sorry. I don't mean to sound insensitive. I'm genuinely concerned for your family's safety."

"No no no." I shook my head although I knew he couldn't see me. "I'm the one who's sorry. This is . . ." I struggled for the right word. "Unbelievable."

He breathed into the phone again and made uncertain grunting noises. "I don't know how you want to proceed. The bank is set to close on Friday. You know how I feel about it but I'm just your realtor. The incident was filed with the police. The house was cleaned. And the bank has given us permission to enter the home and install a security system. You'll have to sign a contract stating you're responsible for the cost of the system and any damages made during installation in the event you're not present at closing *and* also they're not responsible for any other incidents until closing. It means if anything else happens it'll be your dime to clean and you'll be responsible for filing incidents with the police."

I sighed.

He said, "I know this is a lot to think about."

"I've got a contractor lined up to gut the house at a moment's notice."

His end of the phone conversation fell silent.

I had my heart set on the house. I'd built an image of the completed project in my head. I planned on leaving the outside exactly how it was. The house would be an eccentricity. A Picasso puzzle on the outside, a sleek modern masterpiece inside the main house, and an unfinished funhouse—great as a conversation piece and a curiosity—as the attachment. It would be a Winchester house of my own design.

There was a slight ping of sound and I thought it was the front door of the apartment clicking shut. I listened for Eve to drop her keys on the table but the sound never came. I had a moment of panic. I thought Eve might have come home earlier and I hadn't heard her. She could have overheard my phone conversations. I crept to the door, opened it, and listened. I was the only one home.

"Are you there?" Jim asked.

"Yeah." I closed the door and sat down again. "I'm not going to let some crazy dipshit ruin my dream home. I'll sign the contract and have someone install a security system tomorrow under one condition."

"What's that?"

"They have to let my contractor in to start remodeling on Monday."

"I don't think they'll argue with you. I think they want to wash their hands of this house as quickly as possible. You do understand you'll be one hundred percent responsible for the property and anything that happens to it or the materials on site?"

"Yes. I'm fine with it."

"I'll give them a call and get back with you within the hour. Are you sure you want to go through with this?"

"Yes. I'm positive. I want this house."

"Okay. I'll make the call."

"Thanks."

I touched the end button on my phone and redialed Alan. He answered, "Alan."

"Hey. It's Nick. Can you guys install a security system?"

9

I need you to meet me at work tomorrow at four thirty," I said.

I took another bite of wild rice.

Eve stopped chewing. Her mouth was half open and I could see the half-masticated piece of fish she was gnawing on. I fought the desire to tell her to either close her mouth or, better yet, finish chewing and swallow before she spoke. I knew I would get neither and kicked myself for not waiting until she was about to shovel more food into her gaping hole before I spoke. It was the first time in a week she acknowledged my presence and the first time either of us spoke to the other.

She began chewing again and swallowed. Internally I thanked her for not speaking with her mouth full. She sat up straighter in her chair, raised an eyebrow, and slightly sucked her cheeks in. I hated when she did this. This was her 'I was right and you were wrong' expression. Her 'you broke first' expression. Her 'I won' expression. I wanted to flip the fucking table over and tell her she wasn't right and I didn't give a fuck if I broke first because *I* won. I fucking won big and I would always win and we were only a day away from me proving it. And she had no idea what the fuck was coming.

With her eyebrow still raised she asked, "Why?"

"It's a surprise."

Her face softened and she struggled to keep the hard ass attitude. She must have thought I was apologizing. She paid close attention to the fish on her plate and poked at it with her fork, avoiding looking at me. I could detect a hint of a smirk on her lips.

"I don't know if I'll be able to make it," she said. "I have some things I need to do after class tomorrow." She tentatively took a bite of her food and looked at me for a reaction.

Jesus. She wants me to fucking grovel, I thought. She probably thought I planned a dinner or some type of date to make up for how I've treated her. She couldn't be more wrong. I wasn't sorry and I never would be.

"Well," I said. "Based on our previous agreement, which I don't have the energy to repeat, you are required to meet me at my place of business tomorrow at four thirty. And to further cement *you will be there* . . ." I leaned forward and rested my elbows on the table. "If you don't show up tomorrow I won't be coming home . . . ever."

She made a sucking noise and coughed. She cleared her throat and glared at me. "Jesus Christ! You want a divorce? Is that it?" She laid her fork on the table and crossed her arms. "If that's what you want I'd be happy to oblige." Tears welled in her eyes and she wiped at them with the back of her hand.

"Did I say divorce? No. I said it's a surprise. You're the one who's trying to ruin it by being a cunt."

She flinched as if I'd slapped her and gaped at me open-mouthed and teary-eyed.

Why was I arguing this? I thought. *I should give her what we both want, and what we'll both end up getting in the end, anyway.* But I couldn't. I had this elaborate plan to make her miserable and then she would leave me. I wanted her to feel the despair I felt. I was going to have to live the rest of my life with the decision she'd made. I knew she wouldn't live the rest of her life with the decision I made but I wanted to see her squirm for as long as possible. She couldn't leave yet. I thought I should be repulsed with how sadistic and petty I was being but I found it comfortable.

"I'm not going to kiss your ass," I said. "You're pissed at me. I get it. I'm pissed at you. You promised me I was allowed to make a major decision. I've done that. Now you need to hold up your end of the bargain and show up tomorrow."

I sat back and took a bite of fish. Eve's lip trembled. She struggled to keep from crying.

I said, "I'm not apologizing for calling you a cunt, either. I call them like I see them."

"Fuck you," she whispered.

She wiped her eyes again and drank some water. Eventually she picked up her fork and continued her meal. She wasn't as eager to scarf down her meal now, poking it with her fork and pushing it around her plate. Neither of us spoke until my plate was almost clean.

"What is it?" Eve asked.

"A surprise."

"You're not going to tell me?"

"No. You'll find out tomorrow."

"If I'm going to find out tomorrow there's really no reason to hide it."

"I'm pretty sure you hid your pregnancy for a while. You can wait a day."

She thought this over for a second and asked, "Do you want to know about the doctor's appointment?"

"No."

Incredulous, she said, "You don't want to know anything about your child?"

I feigned contemplating her question for a second. "Not really. Oh, wait . . ."

She looked at me expectantly. I was sickened by the glimmer of hope in her eyes. It wasn't a hope I was interested in the baby. It was a yearning for me, or anyone she spoke to, to mollycoddle her and lavish her with attention for being pregnant. Her expression made my guts churn. I wondered how I could have ever gotten involved with a person like her.

I fought the urge to stand up, throw my napkin down in a dramatic display, and hiss, 'You make me sick.' It was the cinematographic thing to do. And the past few weeks definitely felt like a bad movie where no one gets what they want and everyone dies at the end.

I said, "How much longer until the kid arrives and you've thoroughly ruined my life?"

Her face fell. She sighed out of frustration. She sat back and lifted her glass in salutations. She said, "The due date is March nineteenth. I'm still in the first trimester." She sipped some of the water.

"Doesn't that mean there's still time to get rid of it?"

She frowned and didn't respond.

I said, "I guess that means you'll be there tomorrow."

10

I clicked the arrow button on the right-hand side of the computer screen. Another image of the finished kitchen appeared. Sam leaned on the back of my chair and gazed at the images over my shoulder. I scrolled through the photos Alan had emailed me. Sam and I made agreeable sounds as each image appeared on the monitor.

Sadie brayed outside my office. Sam and I flinched at her obnoxious volume. She stood with a squat, sad-faced woman with a terrible home perm whose name I thought was Janice. They huddled around the makeshift carry-in Sadie threw together at the last minute once she'd learned today was my last day in the office. Both women were stuffing their faces with pigs in a blanket and conversing with their mouths full. I prayed Mr. Crutch would walk through. They'd scuttle back to their cubicles with their plates like goblins being threatened with fire if they thought he was within ear shot. I wished they would sit at their desks to eat so I wouldn't have to watch them eat their way to diabetes. I silently thanked any higher power they were far enough away I didn't have to listen to them smack their lips and moan over the cholesterol saturated gruel they called food.

Sadie asked me at least once an hour if I'd gotten something to eat since she'd plopped the worn and stained plastic containers on a table outside my office and pulled the lids off so the food could begin the spoiling process. The first three hours I told her no. But the fourth time she asked I lied and said I had gotten a plate and, because she lingered around expectantly for a compliment, I told her it was delicious. My eyes dropped to Sadie's crusty feet. She wasn't keen on taking care of herself. I couldn't imagine what kind of breeding ground for dysentery her home was. It made my skin crawl to think about it. She was delusional if she thought I would eat anything she'd prepared in her kitchen.

Sam made a confused sound. I imagined he was staring at the two women eating, also.

"Whoa, back up," he said.

"Huh?"

I directed my attention back to the computer. A photo of the living room was displayed on the screen. The image showcased beautiful wooden floors and tall white walls. I was unaware I was still clicking through the photos as I watched the women at the feeding trough.

"Click back to the previous photo," Sam said.

I did as he asked.

Another image of the living room appeared. This one showed the stairs at an odd angle but the exposure of the photo made the room look dark. Normally you would see the black door to the addition in this photo but it was barely discernible due to the poor light quality.

Sam pointed to an area on the opposite side of the stairs.

"Who's that?" he said.

There was a dark shadow half hidden behind the stairs. It almost appeared as if a person was peeking out. The face was completely hidden in shadow and they were wearing some sort of apparatus on their head I wasn't familiar with.

"Don't know," I said. "One of the workers?"

Sam's finger traced the shadow in the picture an inch from my screen. He flicked his wrist in an exaggerated motion to insinuate the lines extending from whatever was on the person's head.

He said, "Looks like horns."

I stared at the photo. "It does."

"Two sets of horns. Like one of those Pagan goat gods or something."

I zoomed in on the figure to see if he was wearing a construction mask I'd never encountered before. The photo became bleary and I couldn't make out anything but a pitch black shadow.

Sam laughed. "Maybe you have ghosts."

I laughed nervously. "I don't believe in ghosts."

Something about the darkness of the zoomed in photo made me uneasy. I reset the image and clicked on the arrow to continue scrolling through the finished photos of the house.

A crescendo of female voices distracted me from the computer. The moment I looked up to see what caused the commotion Sam stopped leaning on my chair.

He said, "Your wife is here."

Sadie and a few of the other hobgoblins were gathered around Eve. The women were talking to her excitedly. Eve was smiling and nodding at them. She failed to hide her confusion behind their sudden verbal onslaught.

Sam exited my office to greet her. I rose from my chair and stood in the doorway. I leaned on the doorframe and waited for the excitement to die down. Eve spoke with Sam for a minute and seemed more at ease with him than speaking with the office trolls.

I noted the dress slacks Eve wore were riding an inch or two higher than her normal waistline. The fabric was pulled tight and there was the slightest protrusion of her belly. *God,* I thought. *She's already packing on the pounds.*

Eve noticed me and a glimmer of anger flickered across her face. She excused herself from the conversation she was having with Sam. The other women continued yakking away to one another about pointless things like television shows and what they were going to make for dinner.

Eve approached me with a forced smile. Once she was in front of me her jaw muscles tightened and she whispered through clenched teeth, "We need to talk."

I moved out of the doorway and motioned for her to enter. She stepped past me and I shut the door. She leaned on the edge of my desk, crossed her arms, and bowed her head.

After a moment of silence she looked up at me and said, "You quit your job."

I tried not to sound smug but it was impossible. "No. I still have a job. I'll be working from home from now on."

She pursed her lips and nodded. She raised her eyebrows as if she were expecting me to elaborate. I was certain what I'd said summed up the situation. There was no need to explain it any further. I was going to treat this the same way she treated the pregnancy when she informed me. She made a choice without consulting me and expected me to be okay with it and couldn't understand why I didn't see things the way she did.

She shrugged. "That's it? This was your big decision. You're gonna stay at home with the baby while I work."

I cringed when she said the word 'baby' but regained myself and laughed a tad too loud. "Oh no. This is just the beginning." I retrieved my phone from my pocket and checked the time. "In fact we should get going. We have an appointment."

I strode past her and retrieved my jacket and a box of items I would need at home from the other side of the desk. Eve pushed herself off the desk and spun to face me. Her back was to the windows of my office so my coworkers couldn't see her. She let her true feelings run rampant across her face when she knew no one else could see. She raised her eyebrows and her lower jaw jutted to the side. The expression made her look like a prissy royal bitch. She might as well have been a thirteen year old throwing a hissy fit over cell phone privileges.

"One," she said.

"One?" I kept a neutral expression for the hungry jackals watching for gossip.

"You're only allowed one choice. This is it. You're working from home."

"That's not the deal."

She looked incredulous and the volume of her voice raised a couple of notches. "I made *one* decision." She held up her index finger to accentuate the number. "You don't get to keep making selfish life-altering choices to be spiteful for the rest of your life, Nick." She spat my name as if it were something foul.

I kept my calm demeanor and sat my box of things on the desk. I smiled pleasantly to placate the worried looks we were receiving from the people watching. "Please keep your voice down," I said. "I wouldn't want you to embarrass yourself in front of my coworkers."

Her face reddened. She stared daggers at me.

"First of all," I said. "I think your decision was far more selfish and life-altering than my choice to work from home. And second, I'm certain you're not going to object to our next stop."

She looked at me doubtfully and sighed. I extended my arms as if I were waiting for a hug.

"Come on," I said. "Let's pretend we're a loving couple for the office gossip."

"Fuck you," she whispered and hugged me.

I kissed her forehead. Her hair smelled like fruit. The compulsion for women to smell like something edible always perplexed me. I wouldn't say it was unsavory. But I found it disturbing. No one naturally smelled like food or flowers or whatever musk man created and put into bottles of shampoo and soap and perfume. I understood some people's bodies didn't smell pleasant on their own but I always found unscented soap and deodorant enough.

Eve pulled away and I collected my things. We exited my office. Eve proceeded toward the gaggle of women gathered around the table of food. I found Sam in his office and assured him I would be back to work once the internet was up and running at the house. I thanked him for not mentioning the house to Eve, shook his hand, and told him I'd see him when I came in for the monthly meeting.

I gathered Eve and we rode the elevator down to the parking garage in silence. Neither of us spoke during the drive either. Eve stared straight ahead with a neutral expression. She didn't bother with the radio which was always set to a talk station. Whenever she was in the car she would either turn the volume down or change it to some cartoonish station that played the top forty in a maddening loop. This time she was resigned and didn't break her gaze from straight ahead.

When I was a couple of blocks from the building I asked, "Aren't you gonna ask me what's going on?"

She didn't look at me. "Nope. You're gonna do whatever it is you want to do. There isn't anything I can do to stop you."

I fought a grin. She wanted me to feel bad about this. The reverse psychology tactic was lame and transparent. I was *never* going to feel bad for what I was doing. She could try to guilt me into submission all she wanted. I felt triumphant knowing she was uncomfortable and she didn't have control of the situation. There wasn't anything she could say or do to change my mind and it made her miserable.

I spotted the two story brick building. It had three nondescript glass doors spaced methodically down the length with small windows in between. I was able to find a parking spot close.

I exited the car and fed the meter to cover an hour. Eve surveyed the building, looking for any indication of what it was used for. Venetian blinds were drawn closed in each window and the doors had large numbers etched into the glass to assure people they were at the right address. There were no signs on the outside of the building.

I approached the middle door and opened it for Eve. She gave me a suspicious look as she cautiously stepped inside and I followed.

We entered a small lobby. There was a receptionist's window. The glass of the window was closed and seemingly locked. The room beyond the window was dark. On either side of the window was a hall. An open staircase was positioned on the right-hand side of the lobby. A directory hung on the wall with arrows pointing to the halls or the stairs. I followed the arrow for the title office and led Eve down the hallway to the left.

The door to the office was open. A heavy smell of cheap perfume wafted into the hallway. I almost choked on the scent and Eve made a small unpleasant sound as we entered.

A frumpy woman in her sixties with a beehive and small reading glasses perched on the end of her nose sat at a worn metal desk. A cubicle wall behind her partitioned her from the rest of the office. She looked up from some paperwork when we entered and frowned at us. I was certain she was the source of the cheap perfume. The woman had deep set wrinkles beside the corners of her mouth. The lines were permanently etched into her face from constant scowling. It made her look like a bulldog.

Her tone was snide. "Can I help you?" She continued to frown as if we'd ruined the rest of her life.

"I have a five o'clock appointment," I said.

She stared at me, unmoving.

"Nick Graves," I said.

She sighed and checked an appointment book on her desk. She hit a button on her phone with more force than necessary. A tone sounded behind the cubicle wall. The dramatic display the receptionist put on, and use of the phone, was unnecessary and annoying.

The person she paged spoke and could be heard through the phone *and* from behind the wall without the intercom.

"Yeah?" the female voice said.

The receptionist pushed a button on the phone and leaned in close to speak. "Your five o'clock is here." The sound of her voice emanating from the other person's phone was distorted and barely comprehensible.

"Send them back."

The receptionist thumbed over her shoulder and said, "Go on back."

I proceeded toward the opening in the cubicle wall. A red-headed female peered over the wall at me. She waved for me to enter her Spartan makeshift office. The woman appeared friendly and gave us a warm smile. She wore no makeup and had a thick spattering of freckles across her cheeks. She was petite and appeared to be in her late twenties.

She extended her hand to me. "Jane."

I shook her hand. "Nick," I said and pointed to Eve. "This is my wife Eve."

I glanced at Eve as she shook Jane's hand reluctantly and wore a confused expression. Eve looked about the desk for answers. The top of the desk was littered with manila folders.

Jane motioned toward two chairs in front of her desk. "Have a seat," she said. She took her chair behind the desk and started opening the folders and rummaging through the folders. "You guys are my last appointment. I got your paperwork all lined up. Let's see . . ." She pulled a stack of papers held together by a paperclip from one of the folders and scanned the top sheet. "Six six zero six Yellow Tree Lane in Edenville?" She raised an eyebrow in question and waited for my reply.

Eve gave a small convulsive jerk. Anyone observing would've thought she'd hiccupped.

Jane's eyes flickered to Eve and back to me. She retrieved a pen from her desk.

I answered, "That's correct."

Jane slid the papers across the desk toward me and said, "Okay. This paper explains you're purchasing the said property for this price." She used the pen to point to the address and price. "Go ahead and read through if you want. If everything looks correct you'll sign here." She pointed to a line at the bottom of the page.

I skimmed the information and signed where she instructed. The next few minutes were spent with Jane flipping through the stack of papers, explaining what was printed on each sheet, and me signing in the appropriate place.

I side-glanced a few times to catch Eve's reaction as all of this happened. She sat stoically with her eyes glazed over. She had the appearance of someone not paying attention and off in dreamland.

Jane halted at a document. She said, "This is the last one and it's for Eve." She slid the paper toward Eve and held a pen out for her. "It states you're aware your husband is making a major purchase in his name alone." She pointed to where Eve needed to sign.

Eve snapped out of her daydream and said, "I'm sorry. What's it for?"

Jane smiled nervously. "Since Nick is purchasing the house in his name, and you two are married, you have to sign stating you know he's making a major purchase." She waggled the pen at Eve. "In the event of a divorce the state wants you to be aware of the other party's assets so they can be divided equally." Jane blinked rapidly and shook her head before she sputtered, "Oh . . . uh . . . n-not that you guys would get divorced."

"No worries," Eve said and perked up.

Jane's face reddened to match the color of her hair.

Eve took the pen from her and said, "I know you didn't mean anything by it." She set her pen wielding hand on the paper and looked at me. "Till death do us part. Right, honey? What's mine is yours?"

I wanted to scream 'Fuck you! I want you to die right now!' but instead I said, "Of course."

I feigned shock at the thought of divorce for Jane's sake. Eve smiled smugly and signed the paper.

PART 2

THE CEREMONY

11

E ve inspected the houses on the edge of town as I drove. The sun was bright and the sky was a clear shade of blue. I drove by the small white church and admired the arched double doors. The structure wasn't something I would have designed but its appearance fit the town. It made the place feel more nostalgic for an era long gone. My eyes followed the steeple extending into the vastness of the sky. The church made the town appear as if a picture of it should be on a post card. Without the church the town was a series of shitty businesses constructed out of corrugated metal and brick with a scattering of dated Cape Cods from the forties and ranch style homes from the fifties. I wasn't a religious person but the town would be fucking depressing without the church.

Eve took in her surroundings stoically. She hadn't spoken since we'd left our apartment for the last time. Her air of calm complacency after signing the closing papers grated on my nerves. I wasn't sure why but I felt as though *she* were the one pulling something over on me. On the ride home from the title office I described the house to her. I told her about all the updating it had undergone. I explained how I'd purchased new furniture and had it delivered so we wouldn't need hers anymore. I told her she had to quit her job because we were moving two hours away and my income was sufficient for us to live comfortably. She didn't say one negative word or flinch as I went over the grocery list of changes. I asked her a few times if she'd heard me because none of it appeared to bother her. Her total acceptance infuriated me but I suppressed my frustration and anger. I wanted the big reveal to cause a major meltdown. I expected a fight to follow once we were out of the title office. The fight would've signaled I'd finally managed to conquer her happiness and obliterated it. I wanted her to be pissed about the move. I wanted her screaming mad because she had to quit her job. I wanted to see her in tears because I was severing the comfort of family and friends during a special time in her life. There wouldn't be anyone to go shopping with her for the baby. There wouldn't be a store closer than an hour away where she could purchase those things. And there wouldn't be anyone to fawn over her as she swelled up like a beluga whale.

I parked in front of the tiny grocery store on Main Street and glanced at Eve to see if I could catch the slightest amount of contemptuousness from her. She gave me a questioning look.

I said, "I threw out the food in the refrigerator. Figured it wouldn't make the drive. This also gives us a chance to check out the grocery store."

She peered out the car window at the corrugated wall of the store. "This is the grocery store?"

"Yeah."

She sighed. "It's kind of small. They probably don't have much in the ethnic section."

"They probably don't have an ethnic section."

She groaned. "How am I supposed to make Indian or Mexican or Middle Eastern?"

"I'm pretty sure you can find the spices and make it from scratch."

"I doubt it."

"Order the shit online then. I don't care. Do what you gotta do." I checked the time on my phone. "Look, we have forty-five minutes before the movers arrive at the house. Get what you can and grab something from the deli or the freezer for supper."

She made a sour face, opened her door, and slammed it behind her in a childlike tantrum.

I mumbled, "Bitch," and exited the car.

Eve stood on the sidewalk with her arms crossed over her chest. She squinted against the brightness of the sun. The stance pulled her T-shirt tight against her stomach. I noted her potbelly and debated on making a comment about purchasing low calorie options for myself. She shielded her eyes from the sun and looked up and down the street. I joined her on the sidewalk.

"Where is everyone?" she said.

I shrugged and followed her gaze. Our car was the only car parked on the street. There wasn't another soul to be seen on the sidewalks. The stoplight at the end of the block changed from red to green even though there were no cars to pass under it.

"This town is creepy quiet," she said. "It feels abandoned."

"It's the middle of the day on a weekday. People have jobs and kids are in school."

"What school?" she mumbled unctuously.

"Can you wait until we get to the house before you start making smarmy remarks?"

The muscles in her jaw flexed. She turned and walked toward the store. I followed her. She threw open the door and the top hit a bell on a spring. The sound startled her and I bit back a laugh.

We entered to find a dated checkout lane situated in the front-middle of the store. It didn't have a conveyor belt but a steel table with a built in scale. A girl with black side swept hair sat on a stool by the register reading a paperback. She wore an unflattering orange vest with black skinny jeans and too much black eyeliner. She chomped away on a piece of gum and reluctantly tore her eyes from the pages to look at us. She gawked for a moment before turning her attention back to the book.

The store appeared to have a total of six aisles. Eve grabbed a cart and headed toward the wall on the right. One of the wheels on the cart made a horrible racket and the contraption pulled to the right. Eve struggled with it but managed to steer it to the first shelf without hitting anything. The shelf was full of condiments and she grabbed a few of the basics.

Eve flipped a bottle over, looking for a price. She said, "There's not much to choose from and the prices are inflated."

"Just get what we need."

She continued to prowl the aisles with the fucked up cart and found a variety of complaints: the spices were lacking, the price of chicken was outrageous, they didn't have any fresh seafood, they didn't carry the brand of paper towels she liked, the produce section was small and everything smelled spoiled, and on and on and on . . . Between the screeching cart and her bitching I felt like killing myself by the time we made it to the check out.

The girl hadn't moved from her stool. She'd lost the book but gained a companion. Now she was accompanied by a stocky man who appeared in his late fifties. His hair was almost completely gray and he sported the large, round belly of someone who didn't bother to watch their diet. His stomach strained against his button down shirt. He smiled warmly as we approached. The girl chewed her gum openmouthed and gave Eve a surly look.

I began to unload the cart onto the metal table. The girl grabbed each item as if her hand was weighted. She slowly swiped the items across the scanner and acted as if we'd inconvenienced her because she had to perform her job. The man pulled a paper sack from under the table and flipped it open. He grabbed each item with both hands and bagged them. He struck up a conversation with Eve.

He said, "You folks passin' through?"

Eve sounded unsure as she answered. "Uh, no. We bought a house here."

We? I thought. *What's this* we *shit?* I *bought the house.*

"Oh?" he said. "Where's about?"

Eve looked at me for an answer. I placed the last of the items on the table.

"It's on Yellow Tree Lane," I said.

The girl froze—her mouth mid chew—and looked at me for a second before resuming her task with more vigor than before. The man didn't miss a beat.

He said, "Oh. I know the house you're talkin' about. The playhouse."

Eve flinched. She looked away embarrassed. He continued to bag our groceries. He moved in a peculiar way and I wondered if he was mentally stunted.

I asked, "The playhouse?"

He grabbed another item and I noticed what had embarrassed Eve. The man was missing both of his thumbs. I pointedly stared at his face to avoid looking at his hands.

He said, "That's what everyone calls it around here. Don't it look like a playhouse?"

The girl told Eve the total. I retrieved my wallet and handed the cashier my bank card.

"I guess it does," I said.

The girl hastily handed me the receipt and removed her vest. She wore a tight T-shirt that revealed firm ample breasts. I tried not to stare at those also.

The girl said in a clipped tone, "I'm going on break."

She didn't make eye contact with any of us as she threw her vest under the table. She spun around to a small cigarette display behind her and snatched a pack of cigarettes before exiting through the front door.

Eve looked like she wanted to say something but kept whatever she was thinking to herself. Instead she grabbed the cart and pushed it back to where she'd found it. The wheel squealed in protest the whole way. The man finished bagging our things and slid three paper sacks toward me.

I picked up two of the bags and said, "What do you know about the house?"

He bit his lip and appeared to think about the question before answering. "Nothing really. Just no one lives there long. And it's for sale more than it's occupied."

Eve rejoined me and retrieved the third bag of groceries.

"By the way," he said and extended his thumbless hand toward Eve, "my name's Adam."

She shook his deformed hand with an uneasy expression and said, "Eve."

Adam guffawed and pumped her hand. "Would you look at that. Adam and Eve." He laughed again and released Eve's hand.

I said, "Nick."

He extended his hand to me. I lifted the bags to insinuate my hands were full. I was grateful I had an excuse to avoid touching the fat man's handicapped paw. I could only think of his hands as paws. He looked like a bear pawing at a jar of honey the he way he worked them to fill our bags.

"Well," he said, "it was nice meeting you, Eve and Nick. I guess we'll be seeing you around."

"You too," I said.

I nudged Eve and we both headed for the door. Just as Eve laid her hand on the handle Adam called to us.

"Oh, hey," he said. "Church services are Sunday at ten A.M."

I said, "Uh, okay." And then I whispered to Eve, "Let's go."

Eve turned to me as she exited and stage whispered, "He doesn't have any thumbs."

Eve didn't notice the girl leaning against the driver's door of my car because she was looking for a reaction from me. She started to say something else but turned and spotted the girl. The girl had her back toward us. Eve's gait stuttered and I almost ran into her. The girl leisurely took a drag of her cigarette. I continued toward the car. Eve followed me. I sat my bags on the trunk of the car and fished the keys out of my pocket.

We put the groceries in the trunk. The girl didn't budge. She acted as though we weren't there. Eve shot me an incredulous look. I shrugged and hit the unlock button for the doors. Eve entered the car on the passenger side and I approached the girl. She continued smoking and made no sign she was aware of my presence.

I grabbed the door handle directly beside her ass and said, "Excuse me."

She took a long draw of her cigarette, turned her petite face toward mine, and blew the smoke in my face.

Rage doesn't describe the feeling that flooded through me. Thousands of bacteria thrived in cigarette smoke and the residue left a sticky film of filth on everything it touched. The girl might as well have spit in my face. I didn't see the difference between the two sentiments. I wanted to wrap my hands around the stupid cunt's throat and squeeze until her face was purple. I wanted to turn her around and shove my cock up her tight, young, unfucked asshole and choke the life out of her. Maybe then she would appreciate the clean oxygen every living thing had the right to breathe. The way I saw it, oxygen and sex were one and the same. You don't realize how much they matter until you're not getting any.

The girl smirked. Her intentional faux pas infuriated me and this amused her. I clenched my jaw and gripped the door handle so hard I thought I would break it or break the bones in my hand. I thought, *I should pull the door open quickly and with enough force to knock her down.* She pushed off my car with her ass, dropped her cigarette on the ground, and made her way back to the store.

I entered the car and slammed the door. Eve flinched.

She said, "She doesn't look old enough to be smoking."

Through gritted teeth I said, "I hope she dies of lung cancer before she's twenty."

I started the car and surpassed the speed limit once I was on Yellow Tree Lane. The movers would arrive soon and I felt like I needed a shower.

12

We entered the front door with the groceries in tow. Eve absorbed the aesthetic of the living room. I explained the updates to her. I told her the hardwood ash floor was stained pewter gray and the walls were painted wickham gray and the trim color was called twilight zone. I mentioned the Karlstad sofa and two chaise lounges in Sivik dark gray and the high gloss black Tofteryd coffee table from Ikea as we passed them. She rolled her eyes at the mention of Ikea and I wanted to slap the ungrateful bitch.

I led her to the kitchen and avoided looking at her as I explained the cabinets were custom crafted from real wood and stained ebony. I had selected a dark shade of gray granite for the countertops and all of the appliances were stainless steel. I caught a glimmer of awe on her face as she took in the massive kitchen. Nothing else mattered to her except the place where she could go and stuff her ever expanding fat face.

We sat our bags on the island and proceeded to unload them. Eve collected the spices, moved them to the counter by the refrigerator, and opened a cabinet door.

I said, "What are you doing?"

"Putting stuff away."

"Spices don't go there."

I walked to the cabinet beside the stove and opened it. As I instructed, the spice rack was located there. I gestured to it as if I were presenting a prize.

She harrumphed, "I don't even get to pick where the spices go?"

I shut the door. "No."

She placed her hand on her hip and stared at me with her mouth agape. The doorbell rang.

She said, "Well, I guess you get to put everything away since you know where it goes."

She headed toward the front door before I had a chance to respond. I retrieved the groceries that needed refrigerated and stowed them in their proper place. I overheard Eve direct the movers to the kitchen.

A twenty something man with baggy jeans and an acne scarred face entered steering a dolly with a stack of boxes with kitchen written on them in black marker. He eyed me dubiously and looked for an area to set the boxes. I instructed him to place them beside the island. An overweight man, who was already sweating and winded, followed the first mover with another load of kitchen items. The two repeated their trip a couple more times. I stored the plates, pots, and pans and put them in their designated place.

The movers grunted and cursed under their breath as they unloaded the rest of our possessions throughout the house. I finished my job in the kitchen and stacked the empty boxes for removal.

Before I could move to the next area to unload our stuff Eve returned to the kitchen. She stomped toward me and waved an object in my face.

"Why'd you buy this?" she asked in an accusatory tone.

I stared at the item she was waving like a lunatic. I grabbed her hand to examine it.

She held a crudely made doll fashioned out of sticks, twine, and different color stones. The head of the doll was a smooth reflective black stone with an X carved for a face. Two white stones of different sizes were attached as breasts and a large red stone with an unusual symbol carved into it was where a stomach would be. All of the stones were held in place by intricately braided and knotted twine.

It was an item I would have never dreamed of buying. I hated knickknacks. I'd told Eve she wasn't allowed to display hers in this house. Only after she cried a fair amount did I agree she could have one room on the second floor to do with whatever she wanted. I had one stipulation: she had to keep the door shut at all times so I didn't have to see all the junk she claimed had sentimental value. I wondered briefly if she was trying to slide one of her dusty old trinkets through some gap in my memory. But I saw the genuine contempt she had for the object and dismissed the notion.

I took the doll from her to examine. "I didn't buy this."

"I found it on the bed on the third floor." She rubbed her belly and glared at the doll.

"One of the contractors must have left it as a home warming gift. Maybe it's from Alan."

"It's a fucked up gift. No one in their right mind would give that to an expecting couple."

I thought back and remembered I hadn't told Alan we had a child on the way. A few coworkers, family, Eve's friends, and the realtor were the only people who knew. My parents were as disinterested in the child as they were with me as a child. Eve's family lived on the East Coast and didn't plan on visiting until after the baby was born. Which was fine with me. Eve and her mother didn't get along and whenever they were in the same room you could cut the tension with a knife. And her friends weren't the generous or caring type. I was sure her friends had forgotten about her since they hadn't seen her in a couple of days. I'm sure Eve had given all of them our address but it didn't explain how the doll made it to our bedroom. Maybe the realtor stopped by and dropped it off. I thought he said something about being superstitious and he could have given it to us to ward off needless worrisome things.

I turned the doll over and tried to find a manufacture's mark or any indication who'd left it. It appeared handmade.

I said, "Maybe it's some sort of good luck charm."

"There's nothing charming about it. It's menacing."

I sighed. "Are you fucking kidding me? It's a fucking doll." I tossed it into an empty box. "There. It's in the garbage. Happy? Why are you so pissed off at me? And why would you think I'd buy that stupid thing?"

She crossed her arms and mumbled, "I don't know. I thought you might've gotten it to mock me."

"You're out of your head. I don't have time to sit around and craft garage sale trash to screw with you. Now, if you're done wasting my time I have to unload the rest of the boxes."

She squared her shoulders and shot me a defiant look. "I don't like this house."

I growled. "Of course you don't. Doesn't it get exhausting to hate everything to spite me?"

"Doesn't it get exhausting being a condescending dickhead?" She paused and then added, "I don't hate everything you like to be an asshole. I think the house has a creepy vibe."

One of the movers called to us and stopped the escalating argument. I didn't want to spend the first day in the house listening to her complain about how much she hated something I was proud of.

The young mover asked where he could find the study. I leaned out the kitchen doorway. Both men stood in the living room. Their dollies contained my books and computer equipment. I pointed them to the study and watched the fat man lead the two-man caravan.

The overweight man's shirt was heavily saturated with sweat. I shuddered. I'd always had an extraordinary fear of fat sweaty people. I don't know if it was the sheer scale of an overweight person that made me think they were teeming with more bacteria than a normal size person but it made my skin crawl. I was always terrified they were going to touch me or rub up against me. Maybe even fall on me and smother me. And I began to worry he might be putting a lot of strain on his heart.

I hadn't had a chance to check the landline to make sure it

was functional. And cell phone service was spotty in the wooded areas. The contractors were here when the phone, internet, and satellite television were installed. I assumed they were all in working order. But it would be my luck for the fat man to have a medical emergency and I'd have to help him to my car or worse . . . I'd have to attempt CPR. I would make Eve preform the CPR. It would be traumatizing enough if I had to touch him and help him.

The overweight man disappeared into the study. The younger of the two trailed behind and caught my attention when he noticed the door behind the stairs. He was overly interested and stopped to stare at it.

I said, "Nothing goes in there."

He looked at me, startled. His face reddened and he hurriedly returned to his job and disappeared into the study.

Eve stepped into the living room and followed my gaze. She said, "Nothing goes where?"

I pointed to the door. She squinted as if she were trying to see a mirage in the distance.

"Is that the addition?" she asked.

"Yes."

She headed toward it. "I wondered where it was. It's hard to see in the shadows."

I followed her. "It's nothing special and it's unfinished."

She glanced back at me. "It doesn't have to be finished for me to look at it, does it?"

"I guess not. But I'm thinking of leaving it the way it is. It's like an enigma and I like it that way."

I opened the black door, flipped the switch on the wall, and stepped to the side for her to enter. She scanned the area and took a few timid steps down the crooked hall.

"Bizarre," she said.

"The realtor was confused too. His best guess was an unfinished bed and breakfast."

Excitement washed over her features.

I cut her off before she had a chance to mention it. "Don't even think about it. I don't want a bunch of strangers in my house."

Her shoulders slumped and she turned her attention to the rooms. I leaned against the doorframe. She walked down the hallway and peeked into the rooms.

She turned to me and said, "The whole thing is like this?"

I nodded and stepped out of the doorway. I closed the door to show her the mirror.

There were moments I reflected on from time to time. I did this because they were definitive occasions in my life. The events were everyday choices or banal occurrences. At the time they happened nothing out of the ordinary screamed in my face to be careful or to step lightly because within a second of time a decision was about to change everything. Sometimes I wondered what would have happened if I would have gone with my gut feeling when Eve looked into the mirror.

Eve stared at her reflection and something changed in her demeanor. It was so slight most people wouldn't have noticed. It was a drop. Her expression dropped. Her posture dropped. As if marionette's strings were severed and she landed on her feet. But at the same time she moved as if she were being forced to walk in the direction she was headed. I saw the same physical reaction in Eve that I felt when she told me she was pregnant.

She made her way to the mirror and didn't take her eyes off her own reflection. She stopped in front of the mirror with a glazed look.

I waved my hand in front of her face. "Eve?"

She blinked and turned to me.

"Are you okay?" I asked.

Something felt out of place and goosebumps rose on my arms. My gut told me something was wrong. Very wrong. The instinctual response toward fear was fight or flight. I wanted to grab Eve's hand and run to the car and get the fuck out of here and never look back. Now I understood the creepy vibe she mentioned before. I broke out in a cold sweat and my bowels felt loose.

She smiled abruptly. "I'm fine."

A second thought hit me and I became angry. "Are you fucking with me?"

She laughed. "No. What are you talking about?"

"How do I know you're not the one who made the doll? And then you make up some shit about the house being creepy. I know what you're trying to do and it's not going to work. I've sunk too much money into this place to walk away from it."

Her eyes darted around and she appeared confused. When her gaze finally landed on me she appeared startled and said, "I got lightheaded."

I hadn't realized how tense I'd become. I forced my muscles to relax.

She said, "I think I need to eat something."

She opened the door and left me alone in the addition. I peered down the hallway and thought I caught a shadow in my peripheral vision. It appeared to vanish up the steps. I stifled a yelp, shut the light off, and slammed the door when I exited.

My heart hammered and I fumbled with the doorknob, trying to lock it. It was a standard interior handle and didn't have a locking mechanism. I would have to rectify that soon.

I mumbled, "Fucking creepy ass shit."

"Where do these go?"

The voice of the young mover came from right behind me. I let out a small yelp of fright and spun to face him. My reaction startled him. He held an armload of pillows and lifted them to block his face and cower from me.

"Third floor," I barked.

He peeked over top of the pillows and said, "Sorry." He backed away from me cautiously.

I ran my fingers through my hair. "No. I'm sorry."

He watched me with trepidation as he headed toward the stairs. I fought the urge to shiver until he was out of sight.

13

I spent all day hurriedly unpacking so the movers could take the empty boxes. Eve hovered with her hand on her hip and couldn't be bothered to lift a pillow. I thought about mentioning how she could help but knew it would turn into an argument since I'd chosen the placement of the spices. I didn't want to be miserable the first day in the house. But I did want everything put away before I went to bed. I wanted to wake up the next day and not have anything to do but relax and enjoy the place.

Eve finally stopped lingering around and disappeared to make dinner and the movers were finished shortly after. The study was all I had left to organize. I paid the movers and gave them an extra fifty in cash for a tip. I knew they would want dinner on their way back to the city.

Shortly after the movers were gone Eve announced the food was ready. The meal wasn't anything remarkable and it made me sad. I knew from a young age I wanted to be an architect. And when I became an architect I knew the day I moved into my dream house it would be a celebration. The reality was I sat at a perfect table with a subpar meal and a subpar spouse.

Eve stared at her plate with a morose expression and poked at some uneaten food with a utensil. This was not my idea of a celebration. It was fucking depressing. I had the sudden urge to tell her to get the fuck out of my house and never come back if she was going to bring the atmosphere down. The whole experience was tainted by her presence.

She said, "I'm tired. I'm gonna turn in early."

It was still light outside. I pulled my cell phone from my pocket and checked the time. She stood and took her plate to the sink.

"It's only seven o'clock," I said. I didn't turn to her.

There was a brief pause before she answered. "It's been a long day."

I closed my eyes. I didn't want her to hear me sigh out of frustration. I held my breath. I knew she was being difficult just to get under my skin. And I didn't want her to know she'd succeeded. I especially didn't want her to know she'd ruined the one day I always thought would hold great symbolism for me. I would not let her passive aggressive remarks put me in a foul mood.

I let my breath out slowly and silently and continued to eat my dinner. She loaded the dishwasher and asked me to start it when I was finished. I nodded without looking at her and she went off to bed.

There was one small creak from a step as she ascended the first flight of stairs. The house was as quiet as a graveyard other than her muffled footfalls. Once she made it to the steps leading to the third story I heard nothing. I made a mental note to send Alan an email and thank him for doing an excellent job.

When I finished eating I started the dishwasher and made my way to the study to finish unpacking. Everything was in its proper place by ten o'clock. I couldn't stand the sight of cables from electronics and spent most of the time tucking those away and using zip ties to organize the slack. When everything was complete I sat in my chair, exhausted.

The computer fired up without any problems and the internet was in working order. I spent an hour answering emails. I sent an email to Sam and told him I was ready for work. I sent another to Alan thanking him for everything he'd done. And finally I sent one to Jim Hagathorne asking if he'd given us the doll.

When I was finished emailing I checked to make sure the study door was locked and returned to my chair. I unfastened my pants and closed all the browser windows on the computer. I opened a single internet browser and typed 'free teen porn' into the search engine. The page filled with the usual shitty sites offering as much free porn as your heart desired. I clicked on the first one, scrolled through the categories, and found the teen section. Rows of photos filled the page. Each photo was a frozen frame from a video. I scrolled through the photos of assholes and cunts and thick cocks shoved into girls' mouths. The girls wore pigtails and peered up at the person fucking them with an innocent expression. Most of the girls looked like the term 'teen' was a far stretch. Some of them looked closer to thirty than eighteen. There was something really pathetic and off-putting about a thirty year-old woman trying to pass as a teenager. One girl in particular kept popping up every few scrolls with the word 'tiny' attached to the teen label. Her face stuck out more than the others because of the glaring metal of her braces. I started one of her videos until she wrapped her mouth full of metal around some guy's fat cock. I was filled with an image of putting my dick in a blender and backed out of the video.

I clicked through a few pages and started a few videos only to stop them after a few seconds. As soon as the girl revealed an extremely hairy bush or a cesarean scar or something that killed the illusion of freshness I would stop the video and go back to the list. It wasn't that the girls were teenagers that turned me on. It was the flawlessness of their skin and the unblemished, youthful appearance of their bodies. I didn't want the girl to act innocent or timid. But there had to be something about her personality that was clean. And virginity porn didn't do it for me either. Maybe some men wanted to relive their first time, or they wanted to conquer and dominate a woman, but I much preferred someone who was experienced.

I finally settled on a video of a pale, dark-haired girl. The video started with her already naked and in full view from head to toe. Her pussy was shaved. She smiled and laughed and turned in a circle to showcase her toned body. The sound was off so I didn't know what was being said. I preferred the sound off. It was one less thing that would make me click off the video. If the girls sounded too fake or annoying I couldn't get off. And sometimes the awful music was too distracting.

The camera cut to a closer shot and skimmed over the girl as if the person behind the lens was inspecting her for slaughter. There was something creepy about the shots but it wasn't off-putting. The video cut to an upshot with the focus on her pussy. The girl stroked the outer part of her cunt and slowly slid two fingers over the lips to spread them and reveal the beautiful pink inside.

I was enthralled with the girl and how perfect she was. She began to rub her clitoris. I pushed my underwear down to expose myself. I'd produced a lot of pre-come. I lubed my hand with it and began masturbating slowly.

After a minute or two of the girl masturbating, the camera cut to a shot of a man getting ready to enter her. I paused the video and backed it up to the girl spreading her vagina lips. I did this a few times, increasing the speed of my masturbation, until I came.

I cleaned myself the best I could with a tissue from my desk. After refastening my pants I slipped out of the study to flush the tissue down the toilet and wash my hands. I was halfway across the living room when something on the fireplace mantel caught my attention. I approached it, confused.

The doll Eve found earlier was propped up in the center of the mantel. I picked it up and turned it over as if I could find the explanation for its reappearance. I'd unpacked everything and was certain I hadn't placed anything on the mantel, especially this ugly knickknack. One of the movers must have spotted it in the box I'd thrown it in and thought we wanted to keep it. I wanted to throw it in the fireplace and burn it but it was late and I was too tired to tend to a fire. I took it to the kitchen and threw it in the garbage bin.

I washed my hands in the bathroom on the first floor. When I was finished I turned the lights off in the kitchen and proceeded to shut off the lights in the living room, with the exception of a small recessed light above the fireplace, before shutting down everything in the study. Before I ascended the stairs I noticed a thin ray of light from under the door to the addition. I couldn't remember if I'd left the lights on in there or not. The thought of opening the door raised the hair on the back of my neck. I would wait until the morning before I went in there again. I was exhausted and couldn't bring myself to deal with any more spooky shit.

I climbed the stairs and left a light on in the hallway on the second floor. I crept up the stairs to the third floor so I wouldn't wake Eve. The third floor was nearly pitch black with the exception of some scant moonlight. I waited a few seconds for my eyes to adjust before I made my way toward the bed.

Eve didn't stir as I undressed. I dropped my clothes on the floor and slipped in beside her. I fell asleep a couple minutes after I closed my eyes.

My whole body spasmed and I jolted awake from a dreamless sleep. It felt as though I had only slept a few minutes. It was still dark and I was drenched in sweat. Eve snored softly beside me. I threw the covers off and groped for my pants on the floor. I searched the pockets until I found my cell phone. I checked the time. It was exactly three o'clock.

Something in the sky caught my attention outside. A few clouds over the woods had a faint red glow about them. The color seemed to dim and brighten in an erratic pattern. The light itself was barely noticeable. But the absence of light pollution helped to enhance it. My first thought was heat lightning.

I slipped out of bed and tried not to jostle the mattress and wake Eve. I stared at the clouds as the light pulsed. I made my way to the balcony doors. The light didn't act like any heat lightning I'd ever witnessed. It was concentrated to the one area and it never completely dimmed.

I opened one of the doors and stepped outside. The night air was cold and caused my damp skin to rise in goosebumps. I wasn't a meteorologist. And I didn't know what caused heat lightning. But if its name was any indication as to why it occurred its presence was out of place.

I noticed a pale light emanating from a cluster of trees in the distance when I stepped up to the railing of the balcony. The light from the trees pulsed in time to the light in the clouds. I wasn't sure where our property ended in the trees or who owned the land connected to ours. I imagined a neighbor could be having a bonfire. Three in the morning was an odd time to toast s'mores but who was I to judge? It was probably a group of teenagers who'd found a place to gather away from adults so they could do who knows what. As long as they didn't burn down the woods I didn't care.

The cold made me shiver. I went back inside and slipped back into bed. The sheets were damp and chilly from my profuse sweating. Eve didn't stir as I settled in. It took a few minutes for me to get warm.

I stared out the window at the light in the clouds until my eyes grew heavy. Right before I fell asleep Eve whimpered and said something in an inaudible whisper. I thought she said 'they want the baby' but I was too tired and my brain couldn't process the words before I traveled to my own dream land.

14

I dreamed I was lost in the woods. The sky was dark but a flickering light in the distance kept my attention. I struggled through the thick brush trying to reach the light buried deep in the woods. The tree limbs scraped against my skin and felt like bony fingers trying to hold onto me. The dream shifted and I stood in a clearing. The girl from the grocery store sat on a fallen log by a bonfire. She wore a hooded cloak with the front open to expose her naked body. In one hand she held a cigarette. She took long draws from her smoke and blew rings playfully. Her free hand worked rapidly in and out of her hairless cunt. She masturbated with two fingers and watched me disdainfully. She added another finger as she pleasured herself . . . and another . . . and eventually inserted her whole hand inside of her cunt. She slid her fist in and out of her vagina and puffed on her cigarette. She never took her eyes off me. It wasn't until her whole hand was inside that she expressed any pleasure in what she was doing. She moaned as she fisted herself.

The dream changed rapidly and I was in front of her, naked. She removed her hand from her pussy but kept it clenched into a fist. She took a puff of her cigarette and lay back on the log she sat on. I entered her and fucked her and fucked her and fucked her but I couldn't take my eyes off her clenched, glistening fist and she blew smoke in my face and I fucked and fucked and fucked her but her cunt was too big from the fisting and I couldn't get off and I just wanted to come but I couldn't. She opened the hand she'd had in her pussy to reveal she was holding something. In her palm lay a bloody and deformed fetus. A smell of defecation and blood emanated from the lump of tissue and it began to wriggle. I humped her loose vagina and tore my stare from the thing in her hand to look at her face. The look of disgust she gave me made me furious. I roughly turned her onto her stomach, causing her to drop her cigarette and the fetus. I spit on her asshole and started forcing my cock into her ass.

I awoke in my bed. Sunlight beamed through every window. It gave the faint illusion our bed was outside.

My dick was hard. After the dream I knew I wouldn't get anything done today or be able to focus until I came.

Eve was asleep, lying on her side and facing away from me. I checked the time on my phone. It was ten o'clock in the morning.

I laid my hand on her shoulder and gave her a tiny shake. "Eve."

She groaned. I waited a half a minute and shook her more forcefully. I said her name louder.

"What?" she croaked.

"It's ten o'clock."

She didn't open her eyes. "So?"

"You've been asleep for fifteen hours."

She whined. "I'm tired."

"You should get up and get something to eat. You can't lay in bed all day."

She pulled the comforter over her head. "Why not?"

"Because it's not healthy."

I moved closer and spooned her. I ran my hand down her leg and found she only wore a t-shirt and underwear. I rubbed my cock against her ass. She groaned again and mumbled into the blanket. I pulled the covers down to expose her face. Her eyes were closed tight against the sunlight.

"Can we fuck?" I asked.

She squinted and sighed. "I guess."

Her shitty attitude made me flash to the girl's face in the dream. Without any finesse I yanked her underwear down. I pulled my own down far enough to expose myself. I grabbed my cock and guided it into her semi moist pussy. I fucked her with no other intent than to get off. Eve made no attempt to participate. I closed my eyes and conjured up the images of the girl from the dream. I realized Eve had become wet and I came quickly. When the last spasm of orgasm subsided I checked Eve's face. She was asleep. I pulled out of her, pulled my underwear up, and rolled onto my back to catch my breath.

I was disgusted with her for falling asleep. It was insulting and angered me. If I hadn't just come I would've rammed my cock in her mouth and fucked her face until she woke up or choked on it.

I got out of bed, retrieved some fresh clothes from the wardrobe, and entered the bathroom. I removed my underwear and found a substantial amount of blood on my cock.

Alarmed, I rushed back to our bed and pulled the covers off Eve. Her panties were still down and there was some blood on her inner thighs.

Eve sat up and squinted at me. "What the fuck are you doing?"

I pointed at her vagina. "You're bleeding."

She looked down at herself. "Jesus Christ." She sounded more aggravated than frightened.

She stood and pulled her underwear up. There was a smear of blood on the sheets. She yawned and headed toward the bathroom. I tried to follow her but she slammed the door in my face.

I stood with my hands on the door and tried to talk through it. "Don't you need to go to the hospital?"

"No."

"You're pregnant and bleeding. It's a cause for concern."

She made a frustrated noise. There were sounds of her rummaging around in the medicine cabinet. "If you'd gone to the doctor with me, and were interested in anything about the pregnancy, you would know this is normal."

"I'm pretty sure it's not normal."

"Some women have their periods through the whole pregnancy."

The toilet's flush was followed by the sound of running water from the sink. I stepped back from the door and looked at the blood drying on my penis. Eve opened the door and glanced at my bloody cock. She gave me a disdainful look.

She said, "I'm gonna shower. I need to borrow the car to get more tampons."

I cringed. "Can you use tampons when you're pregnant?"

"Fucking Christ."

She stomped over to the wardrobe and shuffled through her clothes impatiently. Her pissy attitude when I was showing concern for her safety rubbed me the wrong way. I was in fight mode and I followed her.

"You know," I said, "you don't have to be such a cunt."

She spun toward me. "Either you want to be a part of this or you don't. You can't cast me off like I'm some kind of object and fuck me every once in a while when you feel like it. I've given up everything, *everything* . . . to placate you and to keep this family together." She began to count the items off on her fingers. "My job, my friends, my family, almost *all* of my possessions, access to movies and restaurants, and the joy of sharing the miracle of life." A sudden sob escaped her and she pursed her lips, trying to hold back the tears.

"Don't try to make me feel bad." I pointed my index finger at her. "You're the one who started this shit. I will *not* apologize for what I've done or give up everything I've worked hard for." I relaxed my stance. "We agreed to not have children. That didn't mean I didn't want kids then and you could sabotage me later and I would change my mind. When I said I didn't want kids it meant I *never* wanted kids. Yeah, I don't want to know about the pregnancy. I could give two shits. This is your kid. You wanted it. You can take care of it. It would be no different if you'd brought home a puppy.

You're responsible for feeding it and cleaning up after it." I pointed at her stomach. "This *thing* is capable of doing some serious damage to my sanity."

"Don't call the baby a *thing!*"

"I'll call it whatever I feel like since I had no choice in its creation."

Her face reddened and tears welled in her eyes.

"Look," I continued, "regardless of what you think, I don't see *you* as an object. You're a human being and capable of being severely injured or even dying. We may not feel the same about each other as we did when we first met, or even when we got married, but I can't have something terrible happening to you on my conscience. If I think your well-being is at stake I'm going to be worried. I don't want your friends and family and the people in town thinking I'm some sort of monster because you were having a miscarriage and I didn't take you to the doctor. I would love for you to lose the kid but I won't be made into the asshole that caused it."

A tear slid down her cheek. She turned back to searching though her clothes. She selected a pair of jeans and a sweater and clutched them to her chest.

I said, "I'll drive you into town. I want you to go the doctor's office."

"Why?"

"Because I want to hear for myself your bleeding is normal. I want to look like the concerned husband."

She hissed, "I don't want you in the exam room!"

"Oh my god. Be a part of it. Don't be a part of it. Would you make up your fucking mind?"

She shot me a contemptuous look and opened her mouth to say something. I was tired of arguing and wanted to shower off last night's sweat and her cunt blood.

I threw my hands up in surrender. "All right, all right. I'll sit in the waiting room. Okay?"

"Maybe I don't want to go."

"Maybe you could move in with your mother."

She huffed furiously and bit her lip. I could see her internal struggle. Her relationship with her mother was strained ever since her father passed away five years ago. Her mother was emotionally needy and Eve kept contact limited to phone calls on Mother's Day, her birthday, and Christmas. And even those conversations led to Eve ranting for hours about how much of a horrible person her mother was. I wondered if she'd told her mother she was pregnant or we had moved. I knew the argument was over.

She nodded and took her clothes to the bathroom. I stopped her, retrieved my own clothes, and headed to the second floor bathroom to shower. I stood under the hot water for a long time and stared at the drain. I was hypnotized by the pink water disappearing into the slotted holes of the pipe. I bathed only after the water ran clear.

When I was finished I made my way to the kitchen to make breakfast. I'd eaten half a bagel when Eve joined me. She was halfway through her bagel before she said anything.

"Maybe I should call the doctor first and set up an appointment."

"Do you really think it's necessary? I can't imagine they'd be busy in a town this size. They'll probably be happy to have something to do."

She shrugged. "What if they don't go into the office unless there's a scheduled appointment?"

I had the overwhelming feeling she was avoiding the doctor's office.

"We need to run into town for lady supplies anyway. It won't hurt to check in."

We finished our breakfast and left for town. It was cool outside and the heater had just begun to blow warm air when we pulled into town. I parked the car in front of the grocery store. We crossed the road and walked the half block to the doctor's office.

The doctor's office was a small building and resembled a ranch home. I scoffed at the outdated design of the exterior. We entered a small and equally outdated waiting room. I was appalled by the orange stained carpet and faux wood paneling. It appeared the place hadn't been updated since the seventies.

There were two ugly brown pleather sofas against the wall. One had a large rip in the seat cushion. The exposed foam was disintegrating and stained orange. All I could think of was years and years of children and the senile elderly pissing their pants while they waited for the doctor. The whole room—including the glow emanating from the sickly fluorescent light—was nicotine stained.

Eve approached a rickety sliding glass window beside a battered door. I stood behind her, afraid to touch anything. A nubile teen girl with long blond hair sat at a desk. Her attention was on a magazine lying open on the desktop with a medical illustration of a penis on one page and text on the other.

Eve tapped the glass to get her attention. The girl looked up in surprise, quickly closed the magazine, and slipped it under the desk. Her face reddened. She stood and opened the window.

"I'm sorry," the girl said. "I didn't know there was an appointment today."

The girl wore a translucent tight white T-shirt. It was clear she wasn't wearing a bra. I could see her hard nipples through her shirt. Her breasts were a good size, enough to fill your hand without being too big. My cock began to stiffen. I tried to redirect my thoughts and think about something else. I wasn't sure if the girl was sixteen or twenty-six. It was hard to tell these days. I didn't want to get caught staring at a sixteen-year-old's tits with a raging hard on.

Eve said, "I don't have an appointment. I was wondering if there was any way I could see the doctor today."

"Let me check," the girl said.

She turned and headed for a hallway and I took the opportunity to inspect her ass. Her hips were slim and she had a small round ass and I wondered what it looked like when she was naked and on all fours. The girl disappeared down the dark hallway.

Eve turned toward me and rested her elbow on the frame of the sliding window. I wanted to pull her away and tell her not to touch anything. The place made me want to run home and take a shower.

"What if they can't see me?" Eve said. "Do you want me to set up an appointment?"

"No," I said and then whispered, "This place is disgusting. We should go."

The girl promptly reappeared and said, "The doctor can see you." She opened a drawer, pulled out some loose papers and a pen, placed them on a clipboard, and handed them to Eve. "You'll need to fill these out. The nurse will be out to get you in a few minutes."

Eve took the clipboard and the girl closed the glass partition. Eve proceeded to the sofa without a rip in the cushion, facing the receptionist, and sat. I reluctantly sat beside her, rigid and on the edge of the seat. Eve scribbled through the papers quickly.

I stared at the sliding window separating us from the receptionist. The girl was seated behind her desk again. I could see the top of her head and her eyes. She watched me and there was something very suggestive in her gaze.

Eve had almost completed her paperwork when the door leading to the exam rooms opened. A homely, overweight, middle-aged woman with a surly expression and ill-fitting scrubs beckoned Eve to join her. The hallway beyond her appeared poorly lit.

Eve held up the clipboard. "I'm not finished."

The woman sounded as if she'd smoked a carton of cigarettes every day since she was born. She said, "You can finish them in the exam room." Her teeth were as nicotine stained as the rest of the office.

Eve joined her and glimpsed back at me once she entered the door. There was something in her expression resembling fear. I leaned forward and opened my mouth to say something but the nurse shut the door. I wasn't sure what I would have said.

Something wasn't right. Something was rotten and malodorous about the doctor's office beyond its appearance. The more I thought about it, there was something sour about the whole town. I couldn't pinpoint what was wrong but for some reason I began to worry about my safety.

The receptionist stood and I redirected my attention to her. She arched her back and stretched, extending her arms above her head. Her stance caused her shirt to pull tight against her breasts and the bottom of her shirt rode up, exposing her flat stomach. She stayed in the stretching position and made eye contact with me. She smiled and I looked away.

There wasn't much to look at in the office except two hideous landscape paintings in cheap gold frames. In my peripheral vision I noted the girl laced her fingers together and dropped her hands behind her head. I could tell her stomach was still exposed. I redirected my attention to a stain on the carpet in front of the window. The girl dropped one hand from behind her head and rubbed her stomach.

I only intended to glance at her. I lifted my gaze and her eyes locked with mine again. I couldn't look away when she slipped the hand on her stomach under her shirt, lifting it a little more. She groped her breast and I could tell she was pinching her nipple. She closed her eyes and tilted her head back. She dropped her other hand from behind her head and fondled her other breast through the material of her shirt.

My dick was hard. The situation was absurd. I blinked rapidly and wondered if I was still asleep. No. This was happening. The receptionist was knowingly playing with her tits in a suggestive manner. I shifted uneasily on the sofa to keep my pants from pinching my penis. My brain and my cock were in a battle. I wanted to ignore what was happening but it was impossible. No man in his right mind would ignore a fresh young girl sexually exploring herself. This was wrong on many levels. But what was I supposed to do? Should I leave Eve in a filthy and questionable doctor's office with an exhibitionist receptionist and wait in the car? Should I tell the girl to stop? It was apparent the girl was unstable. What if I asked her to stop and she became violent or loud or accused me of doing something I hadn't?

The receptionist dropped her head and watched me as she raised her shirt to expose both of her firm and youthful breasts. She pinched her hard pink nipples and moaned softly. I whispered, "Jesus Christ." *What's happening here?*

I didn't care if we got caught doing whatever it was we were doing. I groped my penis through the material of my pants and fought the urge to expose myself to the girl and masturbate while watching her play with herself. Her thoughts must have been in sync with mine. She released her breasts but kept them exposed and unfastened her jeans slowly. She shifted her hips from side to side and lowered her tight pants a few inches to display her small black panties. She bit her lip playfully and slipped a hand into her underwear and squeezed a breast with the other. Her hand worked rhythmically in her underwear and her expression contorted more and more into one of pleasure.

I couldn't take it anymore. I threw caution to the wind and leaned back against the filthy sofa. I slipped my hand into my pants without unfastening them and grabbed my penis. I couldn't stroke myself because my jeans were too tight. The waistband of my pants cut into my wrist and made it difficult to do anything. I tried to move two fingers along the bottom of my penis and frustrated myself even more.

The girl's hand worked feverishly against her cunt and her skin flushed. She threw her head back and let out a yelp. She gripped the desk to steady herself. Her eyes rolled aimlessly and she bucked her hips. She withdrew her hand from her cunt. Her middle and ring fingers glistened with her own come. She put the fingers in her mouth and sucked them seductively and giggled.

Lost in the moment I groaned and then panicked. What if Eve heard me? What if she heard the girl? I pulled my hand out of my pants and listened for Eve talking to the doctor. I didn't hear anything.

The receptionist hiked up her pants, fastened them, and

pulled her shirt down into the right position. She waved at me coyly and disappeared into the hallway.

Shit. Shit. Shit, I thought. *She's going to tell Eve.* I didn't want to be the one at fault in our relationship. I liked the positon I was in. I was the faithful and providing husband. She was the betrayer. I wanted her to be the asshole when it all came to an end. I wanted people to ask her why she had left her husband when he was such a nice and caring guy.

The receptionist never returned. My paranoia ramped up. I glanced around the waiting room for security cameras. If there were any they weren't visible. I checked the time on my phone. The episode between me and the girl lasted ten minutes. I debated going to the car again and waiting for Eve. I checked my email on my phone and there was a reply from the realtor. He had not left the doll for us as a gift and he congratulated me on the move and asked how things were going and told me if I ever decided to sell or if I knew anyone who was looking to buy to contact him. I busied myself by replying to his email and avoided the subject of the doll and assumed it must have been from Alan. I replied to a few work emails and was engrossed in what I was doing and started when the surly nurse opened the door.

"Mr. Graves," she said. "Will you come on back?"

I pocketed my phone. "I'm not here for an appointment."

"I know," she replied hatefully. "The doctor wants to speak with you."

I worried the receptionist had told on me even though she was the instigator and the one who should be in trouble. It wasn't like I was an old pervert who'd pulled out his penis and started jerking off. She'd started masturbating in front of me. Any man would've done the same thing or maybe worse.

I asked, "Why does the doc want to talk to me?"

She huffed. "Because you're the husband."

"Oh."

"Oh." She mocked me. "Come on. I don't have all day."

This woman needed to be schooled about bedside manners. And what the hell did she have to do that was so pressing? There were no other patients who needed her cunt attitude at the moment. I wanted to retaliate against her hostility and make her feel stupid but I bit my tongue and followed her.

She led me down a dingy hallway with cracked plaster and peeling paint. There were several light fixtures embedded in the ceiling but only one lightbulb lit the hallway. I wondered if the others didn't work or if they were trying to save money by turning them off. I thought, *God, this place is creepy as fuck. I don't care how sick I am I'm never coming here.* I was worried about the incident with the receptionist and my stomach was doing flip-flops. I expected to hear sirens at any second or an authoritative voice announcing I was under arrest for being a pervert. The nurse stopped in front of an open door at the end of the hall and motioned for me to enter.

I entered a windowless room constructed of shitty fake wood and tired carpet. The room smelled sickly sweet as if someone had burned incense recently. Framed certificates hung on one wall and stuffed bookshelves lined another behind a metal, avocado color desk littered with manila folders and papers. Two plastic chairs were situated in the appropriate place for visitors.

The nurse said, "Have a seat. The doctor will be in as soon as she's finished."

I inspected the chairs and chose the one that appeared cleanest. The nurse eyed me suspiciously and reluctantly shut the door. I tried to calm my nerves and the sneaking suspicion someone had caught the interaction between me and the receptionist. I reflected on the incident and tried to keep from getting aroused.

I thought about how the nurse indicated the doctor was a woman. I had imagined the doctor as a kindly old man who gave suckers to children after vaccinations. Edenville didn't strike me as anything other than a postcard town from the fifties in need of a facelift. If the residents hadn't proved to be so strange up to this point I would've guessed by driving through the area everyone acted out there lives like a Norman

Rockwell painting.

I scanned the books from my seat to keep my mind off my worries. Most of the titles were what you'd expect to find in a doctor's library. The books were large and most were hardback editions. A few tomes contained brightly colored Post-it notes protruding from the tops as bookmarks. The color scheme of the library was almost completely uniform. Most of the books were cream or pastel blue or a dull yellow with the exception of one particular set of three books. My eyes were drawn to the black spines of the extremely worn books. They did not have any inscriptions on the spines. My first thought was that they were notebooks but they were too elaborate and thick, even putting Moleskines to shame.

I contemplated examining them closer but figured about the time I did the doctor would walk in. I leaned forward and thought I could make out some writing on the spines. The ink was so dark it almost matched the color of the cover. I leaned left and right and squinted, trying to make out the titles. I listened for any sounds in the building and again didn't hear anything.

I rose and approached the shelf. The words were hand written. The ink was a dark brownish red. I tilted my head to read the spines: *The Preparation, The Ceremony,* and *The Sacrifice. The Preparation* made sense in this context. The tome probably contained information used before a procedure. But *The Ceremony* didn't make sense to me unless it was some medical jargon I'd never heard before. And *The Sacrifice* was just plain disturbing in this environment. Their worn covers made them look like medical antiques used in the Middle Ages when bloodletting was used for every ailment. I ran my finger down the spine of *The Ceremony*. Whatever binding material was used was soft and unusual. I carefully pulled the book from its home. I found a symbol drawn on the cover with the same unnoticeable ink as the spine text. The marking reminded me of the symbols on the doorframe of the house.

A door shut somewhere. I slipped the book back into its proper place and took my seat.

A few seconds later the door opened. An attractive brunette entered holding a clipboard. She didn't look a day over twenty-five. Her hair was pulled into a ponytail at the base of her neck. She pushed a pair of black framed glasses up the bridge of her nose as she strode in. Her expensive looking heels were soundless on the shitty carpet. She wore an open white lab coat to exhibit a very short dress exposing a lot of cleavage. The two articles of clothing conflicted with each other. Her dress said she was ready to go to a club, not to help a patient.

She removed her lab coat, threw it over the back of the chair beside me, and perched herself on the edge of the desk directly in front of me. She crossed her legs and focused on the clipboard in her hand. She flipped through the papers and addressed me without looking at me.

"Mr. Graves," she said.

"Nick."

She kept her head tilted toward the clipboard and lifted her eyes to look at me over the top of her glasses.

"Nick," she said.

She laid the clipboard on her desk and pushed her glasses up again. She extended her hand toward me and we shook.

She said, "I'm Doctor Elizabeth Paxter." She let go of my hand, laced her fingers, and gripped her knee. "I'm sorry to be the bearer of bad news."

"Bad news?"

She uncrossed her legs, turned to the side, and checked something on the clipboard lying on the desk. She recrossed her legs in the opposite position. Her short dress exhibited quite a bit of skin. If she leaned her ass more to the side I might see the crotch of her panties. But seeing her panties wasn't my main focus. The thing that captured my attention the most was a tattoo on the back of her leg. It was the size of my hand and near the crease of her buttock. The tattoo was a series of lines and random symbols. It reminded me of Tibetan writing but I wasn't sure it was.

She turned her head toward me but kept her body in the

position to show off the tattoo. My eyes bounced back and forth from the inked area to her face. She either wasn't aware I was nearly staring at her snatch or she didn't care. I became aroused and forced myself to focus on her face. I didn't want to come off as an undersexed pervert.

"Yes, Mr. Graves," she said. "I'm afraid it's bad. I don't want to sound insensitive but your wife has had a miscarriage."

My erection deflated. "What?"

The doctor spoke slowly as if I were mentally slow. "She's lost the baby. I'm sorry. I've given her a general anesthesia and performed an outpatient D&C. She's going to be loopy for the rest of the day." She pulled a couple of papers from the clipboard and handed them to me. "Here are some scripts for the pain and an antibiotic to keep her from getting an infection." She picked up a pen and note pad from the desk. She scribbled something, tore the note off, and handed it to me. "I want her to take one of these every day also. It's an herbal supplement to boost her immune system. The pharmacist will know where they are. It wouldn't hurt for her to take it every day even after she's healed. Actually, I would strongly urge her to do so."

I tried to make sense of her writing but was unable to read it. I said, "What's a D&C?"

"It's a procedure to clean the womb and stop the bleeding. A woman can choose to recover naturally but it can take a long time and there's a greater chance of infection. I don't want her doing anything strenuous for a few days and no intercourse until the bleeding stops."

"How long will that be?"

"Usually two weeks."

"She told me having a period was normal."

She gave me an empathetic smile. "That may be so . . . but this time it was a miscarriage. I'm sorry."

"No. It's okay."

I rubbed my eye with the heel of my hand and let out a sigh. Inside I was screaming in triumph. I wanted to jump for joy and run down the hallway and find Eve and laugh in her dumb face and shout, "You tried to fuck me over but now you're fucked because I had my dick tied in a knot and there's no fucking way I'm having it reversed because fuck you you sabotaging cunt I win!"

Dr. Paxter placed a hand on the desk behind her and shifted her weight. The movement exposed what would've been her panties if she'd been wearing any. Instead I got an unobstructed view of her hairless cunt. I thought of the movie *Basic Instinct*. My erection came raging back.

She stared at me, expressionless, and said, "She's not to use tampons until her next regular menstrual cycle. You'll want to ask the pharmacist for sanitary napkins. Also, her ovulation may be out of sync. You may want to wait a few months before you try to conceive again."

I wanted to laugh and tell her there would be no trying again. I wanted to tell her I could see her pussy and it looked glorious. I wanted to tell her I wanted to put my cock in her cunt because this news wasn't bad news, it was the best fucking news I'd heard in a really long time, and I wanted to celebrate and what better way to celebrate than to fuck.

It dawned on me I'd been staring at her tattoo while thinking about these things. I directed my attention to Dr. Paxter's face. She watched me intently for some type of reaction. We stared at each other stoically. The awkward silence stretched on forever.

She made the first move. She removed her glasses and laid them gingerly on the desk. She kept her eyes on my face and grabbed the hem of her dress. She pulled it over her hip and tilted her ass till she was nearly lying on the desk. Her pussy was completely and deliberately exposed for me.

I couldn't peel my eyes from what she was offering. Not only could I see her cunt but her pink anus was on display also.

She said, "Do you want this?"

"Very much," I said without thinking. I wasn't sure I'd spoken aloud or only thought the phrase.

She slipped off the desk and pulled her skirt higher over her hips. She turned toward the desk and bent over to show me the inside of her slit. I scooted to the edge of my chair and gently placed both hands on the backs of her thighs. If this was a dream I didn't want to wake up. I thumbed the soft crease where her buttocks and legs met. I ran my tongue over the tattoo and she moaned. I grabbed both of her ass cheeks and spread her open. Her asshole and pussy were clean and smooth. She smelled like candy scented soap combined with the sweet odor of her pussy. I released her ass cheeks and inserted two fingers into her wet cunt. She moaned louder than before as I slid my fingers in and out of her. I placed my thumb on her clit and began to stimulate it while I lightly fingered her vagina. She spread her legs wider and peered over her shoulder at me.

"Fuck me," she said.

I unfastened my pants with my free hand and stayed sitting. Her gaze returned to the book shelves.

I withdrew my fingers and took in the strange candy smell of her. Normally the come of a woman disgusted me. Women reminded me of slugs the way they secreted ooze. I tried not to think about it when I was fucking. I surprised myself when I put the come covered fingers in my mouth to taste her. She tasted sweet and I wondered if she'd used some sort of flavored lubricant before coming into the office.

I sucked my fingers and proceeded to bury my face in her cunt and eat her. I started with her clit and worked my tongue up and buried my tongue into her wet vagina. I licked her asshole against my better judgment. She cooed and moaned while I worked and kept demanding I fuck her.

Eventually I couldn't take it anymore. I rose to my feet, dropped my pants and underwear, and slid my cock into her. She gasped. I slid in and out slowly a few times before I leaned over her and gripped her ponytail firmly. I tugged her hair to pull her head back and jammed my fingers in her mouth until she gagged. Her pussy constricted with each dry heave and I fucked her as fast and hard as I could. I came quick and didn't care if she had an orgasm or not.

I stepped back from her and pulled up my underwear and pants, not bothering to clean myself. The whole office was filthy and I felt disgusting. I wouldn't feel better until I showered anyway.

She stood and pulled a couple of tissues from a Kleenex box on her desk. She wiped her pussy and threw the tissues in a small wastebasket. She took a few more tissues to wipe the saliva from her chin. She pulled her dress into its normal position, sat on the edge of the desk again, and picked up her glasses. She put them on as if nothing happened.

I looked at the chair I'd been sitting in but stayed standing. I ran my hand through my hair awkwardly.

I said, "You're not going to tell my wife, are you? It would make me look like the biggest asshole on the planet if she—"

She waved her hand dismissively. "Don't worry." She smiled coyly. "Doctor-patient confidentiality. I was administering medication."

"I'm not a patient of yours."

She raised an eyebrow. "You are now."

My eyes bounced between the door and the chair. I wasn't sure if I should sit or leave. My thoughts were muddied by the post-coital euphoria. Dr. Paxter appeared amused by my confusion.

"What medication?" I said.

She lowered her voice and said huskily, "A good fucking." She giggled.

I didn't find the humor in what had happened. I wasn't sure *what* had happened. I didn't perceive myself as a promiscuous person and it bothered me I'd fucked a stranger in less than ten minutes after initially meeting. I didn't feel guilty about fucking her. I was more worried about what sort of diseases she may have since she'd offered her pussy so freely. How often did she pull this stunt? How often did a patient need a good fucking? And why? Christ, I'd licked her cunt without protection.

"You can go," she said. "The nurse will help your wife to

your car."

I took a few steps toward the door and stopped.

I said, "You're real friendly around here. Is there something I'm missing? I mean . . . am I insane? First your receptionist did some crazy shit and then you beg me to fuck you. Are the two of you nymphos? Is this even a real doctor's office? Because I'm expecting to wake up at any moment."

She smiled. "Small town hospitality, Mr. Graves. I knew you were distraught over the loss of your child. I was comforting you."

I blinked a few times and tried to process what she was telling me. It sounded insane. It *was* insane. I shook my head and wondered if someone somehow slipped me a hallucinogenic.

"You can go now," she said. "Don't forget your scripts."

She pointed to the papers I'd dropped on the floor.

I scooped up the papers, hastily folded them, and shoved them in my pocket. I hurried to the door and threw it open. The surly nurse stood on the other side with her arms crossed. I almost plowed over her in my hurry to get the hell out of there.

How long had she been standing outside the door? Had she heard everything? Did she know what we'd done?

"Follow me," the nurse barked.

She led me back down the gross hallway and to the waiting room. Eve sat slumped and sleeping in a wheelchair. The nurse walked behind the chair and grabbed the handles. She bent down near Eve's ear.

She shouted, "Your husband is here to take you home, Eve!"

Eve started from her slumber. She looked around glassy-eyed and confused until she found me.

Eve slurred, "It's gone. Gone. No more mad, Nick. It's gone bye-bye. It was a good thing. No more baby." She waved her arm weakly and laughed.

I was mortified by what she'd said. I waited for a negative reaction from the nurse. The nurse scowled. Someone sniggered behind me. I turned and spotted the receptionist through the glass window. My face was hot. I ignored her.

"It's okay, Eve," the nurse said. "We're sending you home so you can get some rest. You'll feel better in a couple of days." She directed her attention to me. "She's on a lot of pain medication. She doesn't know what she's sayin'."

I nodded. "I'm parked by the store. I can run the scripts in and bring the car back so you don't have to walk far."

"That would be appreciated."

I left the office and jogged across the street to the store. The sign on the outside advertised a pharmacy but I couldn't remember seeing one inside. I found Adam sitting on the stool behind the counter, staring off into space. He perked up when I entered.

He spoke enthusiastically. "Well hi there, Mr. Graves. You look flustered. Is there something I can help you with?"

I retrieved the crumpled prescriptions from my pocket and unfolded them. "I need these filled. Where's your pharmacy?"

"Oh," he said. "I'm the pharmacist. I'll take care of it." He held out a thumbless hand.

I extended the papers to him, unsure how he would grip them. He opened two fingers and pinched the papers. He shuffled through them making agreeable sounds.

"Yeah, yeah, we have all this," he said. "You got your insurance information with ya?"

I pulled out my wallet and handed over the insurance card. "I have to pick Eve up from the doc's office. Can I come back in a few minutes to get them?"

"Sure can."

Before I made it to the door I remembered something. I turned and spotted Adam heading toward the back of the store. I called for him and he turned to face me.

"Yeah?" he responded.

"Can you add some . . ." I looked around the store for anyone but I was sure we were the only two. "Can you add some maxi pads to the order?" My face flushed.

"You bet."

I hurried to the car and moved it to the doctor's office and parked illegally by the door. I held the door as the nurse wheeled Eve to the car. Eve said nonsensical things and giggled to herself. And I tried to act like the concerned husband and told her it was okay and I was taking her home to rest. The nurse helped Eve into the car and huffed as if she were aggravated by my presence. Once the nurse fastened Eve in she wheeled the chair back without a word to either of us.

Eve babbled as I moved the car back across the street and parked in front of the store again. She called me some vile names and tried to slap me. I yelled at her to stop and she started crying. I locked her in the car and ran into the store. I knew no one would screw with her but I'd never seen her become hostile from taking pain medication. I couldn't be sure she wouldn't do something embarrassing or cause a scene.

Adam waited at the checkout with a brown paper sack. He pulled each pill bottle from the bag and went over the instructions for taking the medication. I nodded at everything he said to hurry him along and bounced from foot to foot, trying to show I was in a hurry. I knew the instructions were printed on the bottle and I could figure it out myself. Except for the last bottle. It didn't contain a label. He retrieved a clear glass bottle. It was nothing like the standard orange plastic bottles the other medications were in. It contained clear gelatin capsules harboring a dried purple substance.

"These are an herbal supplement ol' Nana Mary concocted," he said. "They're pretty good. Dr. Paxter likes to prescribe them to the ladies when they feel under the weather." He leaned in closer and whispered, "You know? During their monthly."

"Uh," I said, "Yeah. I know."

I wanted to ask him who the hell ol' Nana Mary was but I knew he would take too long to explain it. I figured I would save it for another day.

He rang up everything and I paid him. I grabbed the bag and walked toward the door. I had my hand on the handle when he called to me.

"Hope to see you at church Sunday," he said.

I said, "I gotta get Eve home," and rushed out.

As I approached the car I noticed Eve staring open mouthed at something out the passenger window. I followed her gaze and spotted the checkout girl from before. She leaned against the wall of the store smoking. She wore a short black skirt with a Joy Division shirt and knee high boots covered in zippers and buckles. She had an oversized pair of sunglasses perched on her face. I couldn't be sure because of her sunglasses but I felt she was staring at me disapprovingly. I hadn't noticed her before when I ran into the store. Eve was enthralled with her.

I entered the car and ranted, "Wish she'd find something more productive to do than wait for cancer to show up with an oxygen tank paid for with my tax dollars."

"She's spooky," Eve slurred. She turned to me wide-eyed.

"Only to the future of our nation."

The ride was quiet for the most part. Eve's head slumped once we were out of town and I thought she'd fallen asleep. When we were close to the house she lifted her head and looked at me.

"You're a happy boy," she said. "The baby's dead, dead, dead, dead. Scraped out with a coat hunger and sucked up with a vacuum cleaner. It was like housework. Dead baby. Happy Nick."

"Fuck you. Shut up."

She burst into tears and wailed like a wounded animal the rest of the way home.

15

Eve slept the rest of the day. She slept all day every day. When she was awake, which was the middle of the night, she occupied the third floor like a disembodied spirit. I'd climb the stairs after I'd finished work to find her roaming the room in her pajamas, listlessly. Other times she would stand as still as a statue on the balcony and stare vacantly toward the forest. Either way it was annoying. I gave up sleeping in my own bed after a couple of nights and took one of the bedrooms on the second floor. She never went down stairs and I had to bring meals to her. Every time I tried talking to her she would stare at the ceiling like an invalid. After a week I told her it wasn't the end of the world and she had to get over it and start taking care of herself.

The day after I refused to be Eve's maid I drove into town to bitch out Dr. Paxter for her participation in Eve's catatonic state and find out what the hell was wrong with her. The meeting ended with me sodomizing the doctor and when I pulled my dick out of her anus it was covered in shit and blood and I pushed the doctor to her knees and grabbed the back of her head and rammed my cock in mouth and forced her to clean off my dick. She enjoyed doing it and her vigor for eating her own shit disgusted me. I left the office with a prescription for Eve's anxiety.

I fed Eve the new prescription which made her sleep

through the day and night. After another week she was out of the pain medication and the antibiotic. She was down to taking the anxiety medication twice a day and the herbal supplement once a day. She began to sleepwalk.

One night I awoke to find her standing in the doorway of my room. She'd turned the light on in the hallway and the brightness hurt my eyes. I squinted to see the naked shadowy figure of her.

"Eve?" My voice was thick with sleep. "What are you doing? Go back to bed."

I rolled onto my side with my back toward the door to block the light from my eyes. She shut the door and slipped into my bed without a word. She spooned me. Her skin was cold and damp. I thought I could smell a faint charred aroma about her but dismissed the notion.

Eve ran her cold fingers across my belly and into my underwear. I shied from her cool touch but didn't fight her. I was hard and rolled onto my back to let her stroke my cock. She shimmied my underwear down below my ass, climbed on top of me, and guided my cock into her exceptionally wet pussy. The inside of her was scalding hot in comparison to her skin and I let her fuck me rigorously. Her wet cunt smacking against me was exceptionally loud compared to the quiet night. She fingered her clit and moaned. When I was close to coming I grabbed her hips and began thrusting to meet her as she came down on my cock. It wasn't until then I realized how much weight she'd lost over the past few weeks. She was as small as the day we met. We collided with each other with enough force I was sure one of us would end up with a broken pelvis. Seconds before I came Eve let out a terrifying scream and something hot spread across my stomach and spilled down my sides. I thrust a few more times until I came. I realized she'd squirted on me by the excessive amount of come.

I lay in the darkness and let the last of the orgasm subside and held Eve's hips tightly against my pelvis. She ran her hands through her come covering my stomach and spread it up my chest. She dipped her hands in it again and rubbed her fingers on my lips. The liquid didn't smell like her. I licked my lips and it didn't taste like her. It was sweet and tasted like Dr. Paxter.

Fear sent a chill through my body. I thought the doctor had broken into my home and found me in the middle of the night and fucked me in my own bed. I bucked off whoever was on top of me, jumped out of bed, and hit the light. Eve sat on her haunches on the mattress and rubbed her clit. Her come slid down my stomach and thighs and pattered on the wooden floor. I pulled my underwear up as Eve cupped one of her breasts and lifted it to suck the nipple.

"What the fuck are you doing?" I said.

She moaned and increased the speed of her masturbation. I noticed her telltale signs of approaching orgasm. Something about the sloppiness and sliminess of her cunt and the fact she was enjoying herself enraged me.

I opened the door and said, "Get out."

Her hips spasmed and she threw her head back and let out another awful scream as she came.

Pointing to the door I said, "Get the fuck out. I don't know what's wrong with you but get out. I'm taking you to the doctor tomorrow."

She scooted off the bed and smiled at me enticingly as she moved. Once on her feet she turned around, spread her legs, bent forward, and placed a hand on the bed to steady herself. She slid one hand down the crack of her ass and inserted her fingers into her cunt. She fingered herself briefly and slid her fingers back up the crack of her ass and inserted her middle finger into her anus.

She fingered her asshole and said, "Fuck me. You know you want to."

I stormed toward her, grabbed the wrist of the hand she fingered her asshole with, and jerked it away. She yelped as I dragged her toward the door. I pushed her out my room and slammed the door and locked it.

I stood by the door and listened. Thirty seconds passed before she walked down the hallway and climbed the steps to the third floor. I waited a few more minutes until I knew I was safe and slipped out of the bedroom and into the bathroom. I showered and when I was finished I cautiously checked the hallway to make sure Eve hadn't come back.

I crossed the hallway in a towel since my underwear were saturated with Eve's juices. I closed the door to the bedroom as quietly as I could. I hoped Eve had gone to bed and was asleep. I was overwhelmed by the sickeningly sweet smell of Eve's cunt when I entered the room. But there was another smell. The scent of something burning. A campfire.

The only clothes I had in the room were my jeans, socks, and T-shirt I'd stripped out of before bed. All my other clothes were on the third floor. I pulled on my jeans, grabbed my other discarded clothes and cell phone, and moved to another bedroom on the second floor with a twin bed. I wasn't about to sleep in the enormous wet spot Eve left.

Once I was settled into the new room I checked the time on my phone. It was 3:58 A.M. I checked the weather. It was forty-six degrees and the sunrise would be at 6:52 A.M. I set an alarm on my phone for 6:40 and turned the volume of the alarm down to a whisper.

Sleep never came. I lay in bed and kept thinking about how cold Eve felt and the smell of a fire and the flickering lights in the woods and how strange Eve had been acting since the miscarriage and I couldn't figure out if she was meeting someone in the woods and having an affair or if she was going crazy. I tossed and turned until the sky began to lighten. I shut the alarm off on my phone before it had a chance to sound and slipped out of bed. I pulled on my socks and shirt. I made my way to the bathroom and took a piss and brushed my teeth and then crept downstairs.

I stepped out the back door and onto the enclosed porch. I was immediately assaulted by the frosty autumn morning. The civil twilight lit the world in dim gray. Birds sang their hearts out as the day began. I rubbed my bare arms to chase the chill away and failed.

I'd hung some of our jackets and a few sweatshirts on a coat rack built into the wall when we arrived here. I took one of my heavier hooded sweatshirts from a hook and pulled it on. I stored our shoes in separate rubber totes with locking lids because I would need extensive therapy if I found a spider in my shoe. The porch was drafty which meant there were spots for insects to enter.

I opened my tote and found a pair of black boots I didn't wear often. They were made out of leather and I couldn't wash them. The best I could do was spray them with a disinfectant when I was finished wearing them. I pulled on the boots and exited the porch.

The grass was covered in dew and in need of mowing. I'd been so wrapped up in my work and taking care of Eve I hadn't noticed the leaves had begun to change color. How could I've almost let my favorite season happen without experiencing it? I cursed Eve and her neediness and her ability to suck everything I enjoyed out of my life.

I pulled out my phone and checked my exact latitude and longitude coordinates. I set a pin on the map application and started toward the line of trees at the back of the property. I walked in the direction I was sure I'd spotted the flickering lights weeks before. I wasn't sure I was headed in the exact location but I figured I would spot something.

My focus was on the tree line. I was consumed with searching for a break and almost missed the obvious path. Halfway across the lawn I noticed a line of smashed grass ten feet from me. The line ran from the back door of the house to the trees. I knew it was the path Eve had taken.

I crossed over to the line and followed it to the trees. It led me to a worn narrow path and into the woods. The woods were much darker. The tall trees still had an abundance of leaves and the foliage blocked a good percentage of the sunlight. Ten feet down the path the temperature dropped drastically. I shivered and wished I would have worn a jacket instead of a sweatshirt.

I walked along the path for what felt like an eternity. The

sky began to lighten more and I was able to better see. Progress slowed when I had to climb over some fallen trees. But regardless of the obstacles the path never deviated from proceeding in a straight line.

The trail grew narrower and narrower. I began to feel claustrophobic. I panicked and picked up my pace. I stumbled over a rock half buried in the ground and fell. I scraped my forehead on a branch when I went down. The leaf-covered ground was soft and fortunately I didn't hurt myself any further.

I stood and brushed the organic matter from my clothes. My paranoia and claustrophobia hindered me from seeing where I was. I'd stumbled into a clearing. The stone I'd tripped over was one of many buried in the ground to form an enormous and symmetrical circle. In the center were the remains of a fire. A few small tendrils of smoke wafted from it. There was a faint smell of scorched meat and urine and something I couldn't put my finger on. It smelled metallic and rotten, whatever it was. On either side of the fire were two backless stone benches.

I approached one of the benches. It was higher than standard seating. It was more of a barstool height. I strolled through the clearing searching for nothing in particular. I noticed a lot of disturbance to the leaf-covered ground as if a group of people were here recently. The ground was wet in some areas and there were some scattered small spots of a red-brown liquid near the fire pit.

A group of rednecks must have come here to drink beer and spit chewing tobacco while roasting an opossum or some other disgusting creature. If Eve was having an affair with some backwoods bumpkin I'd happily tell her to leave. She could live with her uneducated, inbred, backwoods lover in squalor or her mother for all I cared. The thought of her fucking some bucktoothed, filthy wretch made me sick to my stomach.

I took a few photos of the circle with my phone before taking the path back to the house. I made it back a few minutes before nine A.M. I disinfected my boots on the porch and took another shower. I cleaned a small scratch on my forehead even though the skin wasn't broken, only reddened. I didn't want ticks or anything unusual like poison ivy. I could have picked up anything in woods.

I was preparing breakfast when Eve entered in her pajamas. She sat at the table and watched me. I plated some scrambled eggs and toast for the both of us. I carried the plates to the table and dropped hers in front of her with more force than necessary. The jolt caused the food and fork to jump. The fork scattered across the table and fell on the floor while half of her eggs spilled onto her placemat. Eve glared at me when I sat across from her. She picked the fork off the floor and smacked it down on the table. I ate slowly, savoring my breakfast. She scraped the eggs from the table with her hand and dumped them back onto her plate. My face screwed up in revulsion when she grabbed the diseased fork previously on the floor and began to eat. It would figure she would eat like an animal since she'd taken to acting like one.

"Did you have fun last night?" I asked.

She stopped chewing for a few seconds and tried to pretend she hadn't heard me.

I raised my voice. "Who did you meet in the woods?"

She sighed and focused on her plate. "I don't know what you're talking about."

"I'm not fucking stupid."

"Neither am I!" she hissed.

"I'm not so sure about that."

"It's really none of your business what the fuck I do."

I laughed. "Really?" I pointed a thumb at myself. "I work. I bought this house. I pay the bills." I pointed to her plate. "I bought the fucking food. I've been doing all the chores the past few weeks. And to top it off I've been doing my job . . . you know, the thing that pays for all that shit. And what have you been doing? Nothing. Nothing at all but throwing yourself around like a pampered debutante." I placed the back of my hand to my forehead, looked up, and mimicked a dis-

tressed woman. "Oh me! Oh my! I've lost a baby like millions
of other women over the course of history." I dropped the
faux voice and my hand. "It *is* my business what you do. If it
weren't for me you wouldn't have any business to tell me to
stay out of. I want to know what you're doing at night."

She took a bite of egg, pointed her fork at me, and spoke
with her mouth full of food. "If I were you I would shut up
and quit asking questions." A piece of egg flew from her lips
and landed on the table between us.

I slammed my fist down on the table. She didn't flinch. It
took everything in me not to yell at her for talking with her
mouth full. But there were more important things to be pissed
about at the moment.

I said, "I don't know why you think it's okay to act like a
spoiled brat. You're a grown woman. Act like one!"

In between bites she said, "I'm warning you."

"I don't know what exactly is going on here . . ." I gestured to the both of us. "But are you fucking threatening me?"

With food shoved into her cheek she yelled, "For fuck's
sake! Are you *still* talking?"

"Fuck you! You're lucky I'm taking you to see the doctor
and not having you committed or filing for divorce. I took
photos of your little pow wow fuck circle. Don't fuck with me
or I'll show them to a divorce lawyer."

She gave me a smarmy smile. "I don't know what you're
talking about but I'll gladly go to the doctor. I like Dr. Paxter." She continued to eat.

I couldn't be sure if she was being sarcastic or sincere. We
finished our breakfast in silence, glaring at one another.
When she'd finished her plate she left it on the table and announced she was going to shower. I seethed as I scrubbed her
dirty dishes. I debated on leaving them beside the sink, along
with any other dish she used from here on out, and telling her
she was responsible for cleaning up after herself. But I assumed she would let them pile up to spite me. I wouldn't
make it two hours without cleaning them in fear they would
grow mold or attract bugs. I resigned to never cook for her

again instead.

The town was dead when we arrived at the doctor's office. Come to think of it, I couldn't remember seeing anyone from town . . . ever. There were always vehicles parked along the street but no one on the sidewalks. And the cars moved periodically. Other than vehicles passing through town I never spotted any being driven. There were the three weirdoes working at the doctor's office and a haggard, fat, redneck woman with a man's haircut who ran the pumps at the gas station. But whenever I was in the grocery store the only other people in there were Adam and the creepy girl who dressed in black. I'd never seen anyone else the entire time we'd lived here.

Eve and I exited the car. She headed toward the doctor's office.

"I'll be right back," I said.

She stopped. "Where are you going?"

"The post office. We're out of stamps. I'll only be a minute. Go ahead."

She shrugged and disappeared into Dr. Paxter's building. Once she was out of sight I jogged across the street.

The red brick exterior of the post office was in desperate need of new mortar. I was consumed with the odor of mold and dust when I opened the door. The place appeared to have all of the original woodwork and the ancient hardwood floors creaked as I walked across them. I approached the open window for the teller. A small brass bell sat on the ledge with a sign to ring it for assistance. Beyond the window was a small room with a table littered with normal postal paraphernalia: scales, rubber stamps, envelopes and boxes of all sizes. To the right was an open door to a back room. I rang the bell.

An elderly woman who looked like she came with the building shuffled in from a back room. She wore a shock of white hair in a bun and a pink cotton dress with a blue vest. The vest had a few pins adorning it where her breast might have been several decades before. She wore glasses so thick they magnified her watery eyes and one eye was fogged with a cataract. She was hunched with age and her liver spotted skin sagged as if she were beginning to melt.

Her voice was frail. "Can I help you?"

"I need a book of stamps."

"Oh. I suppose I can get you some of those. How many do you need?"

"Ten."

She made a production out of moving toward the table, searching its contents, and retrieving the stamps. It felt as though five minutes passed before she stepped up to the window. She extended her arthritis gnarled hand and told me the total. She was perplexed by my hands as I took the stamps and counted out the money. I noticed one of the pins on her vest was an employee name tag.

"Mary," I said.

She smiled at me. "Yes?"

"Are you Nana Mary?"

"You've heard of me?"

"Adam said you're the one who makes the herbal supplements."

She waved her hand dismissively. "An old family recipe. Do you know someone who's taking them?"

"My wife."

"Ah." She smiled and turned from me and began her slow progression toward the back room. "I have letters to sort. I hope your wife feels better."

I couldn't imagine Edenville had much mail but at the pace she moved I was sure five letters a day were a handful.

I left the post office. The front of the hardware store was made of a large glass window. I strolled by and gazed down the aisles from outside. I didn't see anyone and there was no one behind the counter supporting the vintage cash register. I was about to cross the street and head toward the church when I spotted the creepy girl leaning against the store wall smoking. And like every other time she was decked in all black.

She called to me, "Have you checked the police station?

Or the church?"

I peered at the doctor's office and it didn't appear anyone was watching. I glanced at the church and back to the girl. I closed the distance between us hesitantly. She dropped her cigarette and crushed it with her foot and looked at me expectantly.

I said, "What's . . . going on here?"

She crossed her arms. "What do ya mean?"

"Something isn't right in this town."

She faked a shocked expression. "Really? Wow, genius, you've lived here how long and you're just now catching on?"

"You don't have to be such a—"

"A what?" she interrupted and nonchalantly said, "A bitch? A cunt?"

"You've been nothing but hostile toward me since I've moved here. I don't know what I've done to provoke you. I don't want to start anything with you. I just want some fucking answers."

"You wanna know what my problem is with you?"

"Not really. But I'm sure you're going to tell me."

She clenched her jaw. "God! You're making it really fucking difficult for me to be nice to you."

I put my hands in my pockets and shrugged. I checked for faces peeping at us from the doctor's office. The girl's eyes traced my line of sight.

She said, "Don't worry. You won't get in trouble. You're the golden boy now." She pulled another cigarette from her pack and lit it. She exhaled the smoke before continuing. "You're such a sheep." She shook her head in disgust. "And a man. That's what your problem is. Always thinkin' with your dick. I'm not surprised it's taken you this long to think there's something wrong."

"Well then. If you're just going to smoke and make condescending remarks . . ." I pointed across the street. "I'm gonna head back over to the doc's office." I turned to leave.

"Wait," she said.

I stopped.

She drew from her cigarette. The smoke garbled her voice as she spoke, "I don't like people getting hurt." She blew the rest of the smoke in my direction. "I also don't like when people walk into the whole thing like a mindless zombie that's got no choices. You have a choice. You *never* have to do what other people expect of you."

"Walk into what?"

"Mr. Graves!" a voice called from across the street. The receptionist stood in the door of the doctor's office waving her arm above her head to get my attention. She wore a mini sundress that not only didn't seem appropriate for the cool weather but was obscenely short. When she waved the hem lifted to expose she wasn't wearing underwear.

I thought, *What do people have against underwear in this town?* The idea of women's bare genitalia touching the seats of every chair they sat in made me cringe. How could people bring themselves to sit anywhere without getting vagina germs on them?

The receptionist continued to wave and flaunt her vagina. "Mr. Graves, the doctor needs to speak with you!"

The creepy girl rolled her eyes. "Jesus, you're already in over your head." She waved her hand at me in a dismissive manner. "Run along, sheep. You better get going."

I said, "What do you know?"

"I know you need to quit fucking them and get the hell out of this town. The sooner the better. If I were you I'd leave right now."

My face screwed up in confusion. How did she know I was fucking the doctor?

I said, "If it's so terrible why are you still here?"

She fake pouted and said in an exaggerated sad voice, "Because I've got no place to go." She rubbed the corner of her eye with one knuckle. "Boo hoo. Let me go cry a river."

The receptionist cupped her hands to her mouth. "Mr. Graaaaaaves!"

The smoking girl watched the receptionist and made an annoyed sound. She said, "Oh, and if your wife is taking the herbs . . . leave her." She dropped her cigarette without crushing it and headed toward the store entrance.

"Wait!" I said.

She ignored me and opened the door causing the bell to jingle. The receptionist stepped out of the doorway and started toward me.

I called to the creepy girl before she entered the store. "What's your name?"

She paused. "Does it matter?" She smiled broadly, threw her head back, and kicked up one leg behind her as if she were exiting theatrically from a Broadway play.

She didn't give me time to respond before she disappeared into the store. The receptionist was halfway across the road when I turned and joined her. We walked beside each other back to the doctor's office.

"I didn't think you heard me," she said. "The doctor wants to speak with you."

"I heard you."

"Oh." She looked over her shoulder at the store. She whispered, "You shouldn't talk to Morgan."

"Why?"

We'd reached the door and I held it open for her.

She stopped outside the door and shrugged. "She's really mean and a little crazy." She twirled her finger by her ear in the universal sign of lunacy. "She thinks everything is a conspiracy. Like, the whole town is out to get her or something. I don't think she has a nice bone in her body."

She entered the office and led me to the room where Dr. Paxter kept her desk and library. The receptionist informed me the doctor would join me in a couple of minutes. I took a seat and stared at the black books on the shelf, debating on stealing them, until the doctor arrived. She wore her lab coat closed and buttoned today in a professional manner. She took her chair behind the desk.

"There's nothing wrong with your wife," she said. Her mannerisms were clinical and cold. She leaned forward, laced her fingers, and set her hands on the desk with her elbows extended to her sides. "A miscarriage can be traumatizing and each woman deals with the emotional aspect differently. She needs time to process what's happened. And her hormones are unbalanced as her body realizes it's no longer pregnant." She sat back and dropped her hands from the desk.

"How much more time does she need? I've been waiting on her hand and foot without an ounce of appreciation. In fact, I think she despises me more than ever."

"She's expressed she doesn't feel loved. Or physically appealing. It might help if you initiated sex instead of her having to take it from you."

I laughed. "Take it from me? I'm not an unwilling participant. I'm pretty much ready to go any minute."

"Good." She smiled. "As her doctor, and yours, I have both of your well-being in mind. I want both of you to be healthy." She stood and made for the door. "Could you follow me please?"

"Where are we going?" I stood.

This was usually the moment we stole away to fuck. And we always did it in this room. Maybe she wanted to mix things up a bit. The anticipation of sex made my cock hard.

"I want to make sure your sexual health is good." She opened the door. "It's my job. I want to make sure the problem isn't physical on your part." She stepped out into the hallway. "Now if you'll follow me . . ."

I did as I was told. She led me down the dark hallway to a door at the end. She opened the door for me and I entered before I had time to process the room's contents. The doctor entered behind me and shut the door. The room was a worn exam room with a pastel blue sink, coral metal cupboards, and a battered Formica countertop. There was one exam table and on it was the receptionist, naked, with her feet in the stirrups and her legs splayed open to exhibit her fresh pink pussy. Her cunt was adorned with a thin strip of blond hair above the clit. She had one arm under her leg, working a glass dildo in and out of her wet cunt. The dildo opened her vagina

148

as it entered and since it was made of glass I could see inside her. I could distinguish the pink flesh of her insides for a few inches then further in her it faded into a black abyss. It was disturbing. I wasn't sure I liked seeing inside her or if it disgusted me. On the surface there was something clinical about it but deep down a part of me would've loved to dissect her and fuck her organs. The receptionist's other hand slowly rubbed her clit. She moaned. Her eyes were half closed and through the slits she watched for some reaction.

Dr. Paxter stepped around me and slid her heels off. She turned toward me, unbuttoned her lab coat, and dropped the coat to the floor to expose her naked body. She climbed on the exam table above the receptionist's head and straddled the girl so her cunt was an inch above her mouth. The girl eagerly began to eat Dr. Paxter's pussy while working the dildo in and out of herself more rapidly.

The doctor rocked her hips as the girl sucked her clit. I could see come on the girl's chin as she moaned and ate the vagina in front of her.

Dr. Paxter pinched her own nipples. "Come on. Don't you want to fuck Lauren? If you don't, I will." She leaned forward and placed her elbows on either side of Lauren's hips. The girl continued to eat her while the doctor licked the girl's clit. "She's so sweet. Like a peach."

I wasn't sure if the vagina I smelled was the doctor's or if Lauren's vagina smelled exactly like the doctor's—and now Eve's—vagina. The doctor took the dildo from Lauren. She began to work it into Lauren's anus while fingering her clit and licking the come from her slit.

I disrobed while watching them and stepped up to the table between Lauren's legs. I stroked myself and watched the doctor eat the girl, sodomize her with the dildo, and receive her own oral pleasure. The two moaned out of sync. Quickly, I could feel the beginning of an orgasm. I released my cock as to not come before I had the chance to fuck one of them. Dr. Paxter's hair fell in the way. I grabbed it and lay it back over her shoulder. She pulled away from the girl's clit and took my cock in her mouth, looking up at me. I grabbed the back of her head and guided her further down the shaft of my dick. Only after she'd taken all of me in did she gag. I held her head steady and fucked her mouth while she continued to slide the dildo in and out of Lauren's anus. I stopped when I felt the beginning of the orgasm again.

The doctor's eyes were watery from gagging. She wiped the spit from her chin and said, "What are you waiting for? Fuck her."

The doctor pulled the dildo from Lauren's ass but kept the tip pushed against her anus. I entered Lauren and began fucking her. I couldn't help but moan. Her cunt was tight.

The doctor inserted the dildo into Lauren's anus as I fucked her. I could feel it press against the underside of my cock as she tried to match the rhythm of my fucking. The sensation was unusual and excited me.

The doctor made a pained face. "Oh god! I'm coming." She moaned and ground her pelvis against the receptionist's face.

The visual sent me into my own orgasm. I came hard and hollered out of ecstasy. I continued to pump into the girl as the wave of pleasure subsided and I caught my breath. The doctor giggled and began to masturbate Lauren violently. A minute later the girl called out in her own pleasure with her face buried in the doctor's pussy. My cock was still inside Lauren and semi hard. Her pussy constricted when she came. I withdrew from her and slapped her clit with my cock a few times. When I was finished the doctor spanked Lauren's cunt with three hard slaps. Lauren bucked her hips and squealed.

The doctor said, "You like that? You want some more of that, you horny cunt?"

The doctor slapped Lauren's clit a few more times and laughed. Lauren begged her to stop. The doctor began to lovingly pet Lauren's pussy and the receptionist cooed. I knew we were finished and gathered my clothes.

The doctor climbed off Lauren unceremoniously and grabbed a few paper towels from a wall dispenser and tossed them on Lauren's stomach. The receptionist cleaned her face and her pussy before standing. The doctor washed her face in the sink. And Lauren dropped to her knees in front of me. I held my clothes and watched her as she sucked her own come from my flaccid penis.

The doctor began to dress and we followed her lead. Lauren left Dr. Paxter and I alone in the exam room.

Dr. Paxter said, "Everything is in working order. Now for the prostate."

My heart skipped a beat. I waved my hand dismissively. "No no. I'm good."

"We really should check it." She pulled a pair of latex gloves on.

I'd never had anything inserted into my ass and I didn't want to start now. Nervously, I backed toward the door. "Maybe another time."

"Are you sure? We're already here. It will only take a second."

I grabbed the door knob and opened it. "I really need to get home and finish up a project I'm working on."

I rushed down the hallway and into the waiting room. Lauren looked up from a magazine with a huge smile when I entered. I hurriedly told her to send Eve out to the car once she was finished. I was out the door before she could respond. Eve was already waiting in the car. Her appearance startled me. I was sweating and flush and probably smelled like vagina. I'd wanted a few minutes to compose myself before having to interact with her.

I slid in behind the driver's seat, started the car, pulled out of the parking spot quickly, and sped toward home.

Eve said, "Slow down! You're driving like a maniac."

"It's not like there're any cars to get into an accident with."

She eyed me suspiciously. "What took so long? And why are you all sweaty?"

I told her a half truth. "Dr. Paxter gave me a physical and tried to give me a prostate exam."

Eve laughed hard for longer than necessary. She laughed until she produced tears.

I said, "It's not funny."

"Yeah." She giggled. "It is."

"She wanted to examine me because you told her I don't find you attractive. You know that's bullshit. I haven't bothered trying to fuck you because you've been acting weird."

"It's called grief, Nick. And it's apparently an emotion, along with guilt. You know? The emotion you're unable to feel."

"What's that supposed to mean?"

"I don't know. You tell me." She stared out the window at the fall foliage.

"I'm not going to play your psychoanalytic game. I refuse to fall into a lingual trap because of some scenario you've conjured in your head."

She said harshly, "I'm not trapping you."

"Really? That's a surprise."

I pulled into our driveway and took in the view of the expansive house with the woods as a backdrop. The hues of red, orange, yellow, and brown made the house appear grotesque somehow. My own home frightened me for some reason. It looked as if a group of teenagers slapped it together to make a haunted house so they could charge their friends admission to enter it.

I parked the car and said, "I don't want you to see Dr. Paxter anymore."

"What? That's stupid. She's right in town. And I like her."

"I think she's a quack."

"Why? Because she's on my side? Jesus . . . It's always about you, isn't it? It doesn't matter what I want. It never will."

She threw open the car door and stomped into the house. I gave her a few minutes to disappear up the steps like she always did before I left the vehicle. I slipped my sneakers off once I was inside and dropped them in the washer before making my way toward the study.

Something compelled me to stop by the stairs and I stared at the door to the addition. *The Playhouse.* For some reason the name sounded ominous now. Maybe the spirit of Halloween was beginning to sink in with the changing of the seasons. I cautiously approached the addition's door, opened it, and stepped inside. There was a cloying odor of roses and something musky like a wet dog in this part of the house. My mind flashed back to the thing the realtor discovered. I proceeded to check the rooms, searching for the source of the smell. Everything was like before until I reached the second floor.

One of the rooms had a tiny pile of brown powder the size of a quarter on the floor. I stooped and rubbed it between my fingers. It was finer than sawdust and slightly gritty. I smelled the smudge on my fingers. It smelled like roses. I inspected the ceiling above the pile of dust for any cracks. There were none. It was disconcerting and I told myself it was all in my head and I was making nothing into something sinister.

I continued to check the remaining rooms and didn't find anything else out of the ordinary. When I proceeded back to the first floor I found the door to the main part of the house closed. I gazed at my confused expression in the mirror and tried to remember if I'd shut the door. I didn't think I had. The addition gave me the willies ever since we'd moved into the house. And it pissed me off that part of my own home upset me enough to never enter it. I left the addition and made a mental note all the lights were off.

The main house was quiet. I washed the powder off my hands and went to the study to finish a work project. Mr. Crutch would want to review it by Friday and have me make any amendments before the end of next week. I wanted to relax over the weekend because I had to get up early Monday and meet with the client. They wanted to review the blueprints in person.

The rest of the day I was engrossed in my work. I took a brief break to make dinner for one, ate it quickly, cleaned my dishes, and returned to my work.

When everything was finalized it was dark outside. I

emailed the blueprint to the office and proceeded to watch a copious amount of porn. I'd discovered a new site specializing in edgy teen girls. It wasn't normally my type of thing. But there was something about the girls with black hair and tattoos and piercings that felt fresh and new to me. And these girls were more eager to please their partner or partners. One woman was nearly covered in tattoos from the neck down. The teen label was a stretch for her. She appeared angry, yelling at her partner to fuck her in the ass, and squirted multiple times in one session from sodomy alone. The squirting left her and her partner soaked in come. Their fucking produced a loud slapping sound as their wet skin made contact. The hairy man rammed his cock into her ass like a jackhammer. I was enthralled with the woman and jerked off to her angry face as she was being sodomized. When I was finished I cleaned my come with a tissue and left the study to wash my hands.

Away from my office I noticed the house was not quiet. I could hear the sound of grunting and a woman cooing in pleasure. Someone spoke with an authoritative voice. I thought I'd left a browser open and the sound on on my computer for a second but knew I'd closed everything and cleared my browser. I listened carefully and was sure the noise was coming from the addition.

Confused, I crept toward the hidden door. The sounds grew louder. And with the house darkened I could perceive light spilling out from the crack at the bottom of the doorway.

Eve's unmistakable voice called for someone to fuck her harder. Is this where she ran off to at night? Was she having an affair right under my nose? In *my* house? As much as my sudden fury pushed me to throw the door open and storm in to find her fucking some redneck and grab her by a handful of her hair and drag her through *my* home and throw her naked ass out into the cold and slam and lock the door in her face I forced myself to be composed and quietly opened the door and stepped in.

I was surrounded by the obvious sounds of fucking. I detected several couplings happening simultaneously. I tiptoed to the first room and peeked around the doorframe, hoping I wouldn't be noticed. Lauren was on all fours with a red triangle pillow under her stomach to support her hips and keep her in position. A man I'd never seen before was on his knees behind her. He was sweaty and red-faced with long stringy hair and a massive beer gut and he fucked Lauren with everything he had. The thought of a pretty young girl like Lauren letting such a disgusting exhibit of a man fuck her made me feel ill and angry. When the man repurchased his grip on Lauren's hips to drive into her better I noticed his thumbs were missing exactly like Adam's.

An arm flashed in front of my face and I was suddenly in a headlock. The person dragged me from the doorway. Their grip was strong and made it difficult to breathe. They tightened their arm around my throat and I was unable to get any air. I pulled on the unrelenting arm. My face felt as if it were swelling with blood. Dr. Paxter appeared on my left, naked. She held a syringe filled with a milky substance. The person choking me picked me up off the ground. I kicked wildly and clawed at their suffocating grip. Black spots danced in my vision.

Dr. Paxter said, "Don't worry. It's almost over."

She jabbed the needle into my leg. I tried to scream but it was futile without the ability to draw air. My vision dimmed and seconds later my muscles turned to jelly. My arms dropped to my sides. I tried desperately to move them but the connection from my brain to my limbs was severed. The person holding me let go. I sucked in as much air as I could. I coughed weakly and my lungs were on fire. I was a paralyzed fish out of water. My entire body tingled. I was set on my feet but my legs wouldn't work. Swimming black spots appeared in my peripheral vision again. Everything became blurry. I opened my eyes wider, hoping it would keep me from slipping into the unconsciousness I knew was close to consuming me. The person who choked me laid me on the floor. The volume of the world was turned down. Multiple sex acts continued uninterrupted in the addition.

The doctor said, "Get him prepped."
Adam said, "Will do."
I sucked in air to scream but darkness closed in and I was gone.

PART 3

THE SACRIFICE

16

Chaos and pain. These were the components of my existence. I couldn't make sense of what was happening beyond the borders of my thoughts. I knew something hectic was happening but couldn't place where I was or why I was there. When the pain started a part of my brain screamed something was wrong. I wanted to wake but my eyelids were weighted and difficult to open. When I did manage to pry my eyes open everything was a blur of lights and shadowy figures. Silhouettes hovered between me and an overhead light. And as soon as my eyes were shut I slipped comfortably back into the nothingness of sleep.

The sound of a power tool jolted me awake along with an unexplainable pain. But complete wakefulness and a comprehending state weren't possible. Sleep was easy. It was hard to be a part of a world full of chaos and pain. Time no longer existed. The few seconds I was alert I knew I didn't want to participate in my surroundings and hoped the darkness and nothing of sleep was my new existence from this point forward. Nothingness was comfortable. There were no requirements or expectations in the abyss.

Something hit my cheek rapidly and jostled my head. My mind processed the sensation. Someone was slapping me lightly to wake me. I forced my eyes open and tried to focus.

The world was filled with light that hurt my eyes and the smell of cotton candy and feces and roses. The intermingled scents made my stomach roll. My tongue was dry and stuck to the roof of my mouth. I found sleep a better option and shut my eyes.

"Wake up, Nick. We don't have all night."

Dr. Paxter leaned over me and blocked the light from the ceiling and I was able to open my eyes without any pain. She slapped my cheek rapidly again. Her naked breasts moved like pendulums with the movement. I lay on something hard. My back was sore. Pain shot through my wrists and forearms and ached all the way up to my elbows. I tried to move but was restrained to whatever I lay on. I groaned and fixed my eyes on the doctor. I knew from the unfinished walls I was in the addition of my house.

Dr. Paxter smiled. "You're awake."

"What's going on?" My voice sounded weak and slurred.

She laughed and someone grunted and huffed rhythmically nearby. I lifted my head and searched the room for the sound. A breeze brushed my body and buttocks. I inspected the uncomfortable table I was strapped to. I was naked and tied to a mover's hand truck with rope. My backside was sandwiched between two support bars that made the back of the cart. My wrists were bound to the side rails. But the most notable thing was the large bandages of gauze covering both of my hands. The recognition caused adrenaline to surge through my body. My stomach lurched. The fogginess smothering my thoughts vanished and in an instant I was completely alert. My vision became crystal clear.

I pulled my arms tight against the ropes and screamed partly from frustration but mainly from pain. Dr. Paxter tried to soothe me by petting my head. I screamed in her face. Grunting emanated from the corner of the room. The doctor was obstructing my view and I couldn't see what was happening although I had a good idea from the sounds.

I asked, "What did you do to me?" I ignored the pain and struggled against the ropes. "Let me go."

"It's okay." She began to caress my flaccid cock. "It's part of the ceremony. I know you're angry now but once you understand your part you'll come around."

"I don't know what you're talking about." I looked down at her hand stroking my dick. "Get your fucking hands off me!"

"All his male drones must be altered for the ultimate plan to succeed."

"You're a fucking crazy cunt. Untie me." I pulled my arms tight against the ropes again and yelled when I felt pain. "What did you do?"

She continued to caress my dick and it began to stiffen. I was confused and enraged that my body would betray me in this situation. I didn't want to fuck her. I wasn't remotely aroused. I wanted to slap the shit out of her and kick her out of my house and call the police. But my cock was beyond my control. It became more erect as she primed me.

I shouted, "Stop it! Get away from me you crazy bitch!"

My dick had become fully erect and the sensation was nearly painful. She smiled at me coyly and straddled the cart I was strapped to. She proceeded to lower her wet cunt onto my cock. I wiggled as much as the restraints allowed, trying to get away from her. It was useless. I growled out of frustration and let loose a string of profanities that sounded more like gibberish. She placed her hands on my chest for leverage and began to fuck me.

She said, "Removing the thumbs discourages masturbation. After all, you are a man. You have to save yourself for our lord's purposes *only*." Her words were broken by her thrusts. She panted from the exertion and a thin layer of sweat formed over her body. "Don't worry. You can have any woman you want. The lord requires us to mate as much as possible until his conception has reached the required number."

What she was saying didn't make any sense. I was stuck on the first thing she'd said to me. *Removing the thumbs discourages masturbation.* Something inside of me snapped when the realization hit me. This psychotic woman had removed my thumbs. My muscles seemed to liquefy and tremble. I tried desperately to pull my shit together. I began to gulp air and was afraid of going into shock.

I stared at the ceiling while the doctor fucked me and tried to make sense of the situation. I was exhausted but knew I had to stay alert. The grunting from the corner of the room was accompanied with a wet smacking. I lifted my head and peered around the doctor. Eve was on all fours in the corner. Adam was behind her. They were both covered in sweat. Adam fucked her with the gusto of a teenager. His rotund belly slapped Eve's ass with each thrust. She bit her lip and reached in between her legs to furiously rub her clit. She moaned when Adam's grip slipped from her waist. He found purchase again with his thumbless hands and began fucking her harder than before. She begged him to fuck her harder and yelled at him to shove a finger in her anus.

I shouted, "You sick fucks!"

Dr. Paxter continued to bob frantically and pant from the exertion. I bucked my hips left and right but it was useless. The cart rattled but the doctor kept me from flipping it over. The struggle caused unbearable pain in my hands. My vision swam and I thought I might pass out from the pain. I stared at my bandaged hands and tried to ignore Dr. Paxter. I hoped fury would cause my dick to go limp.

I wiggled my remaining fingers and my stomach sank. The newly cemented reality made me feel sick. My thumbs were gone. My vision went red. I could feel my heartrate in my temples.

I screamed, "I'll fucking kill you!"

Without warning I came. The sensation was intense and ran deep into my gut and anus. The feeling made my eardrums tingle and almost made me vomit. My body tensed and I gasped at the suddenness of the release. The doctor cooed in pleasure and continued to rock her hips until I relaxed. She giggled and slapped my cheek playfully.

"See?" she said. "It's only as bad as you make it. Most

men would kill to fuck to their heart's content."

Adam continued to rail Eve in the corner. The doctor stood and stepped over me. She walked behind me and out of my line of vision. Besides the sounds of Adam fucking my wife there was a metal jingling noise from whatever the doctor was up to. I tried my hardest to tilt my head to see what she was doing but being tied to the cart hindered a lot of movement. After a minute the doctor walked past me and toward the couple fucking on the floor. She now wore a large shiny black strap on dildo. The leather straps of the apparatus were cinched tight around her waist and under her buttocks. Semen oozed down the inside of her thigh and I gagged. I never had the stomach to watch cream pies.

I yelled to be let go and the doctor threatened to gag me if I didn't shut up. Adam slowed his pace when the doctor stood behind him. He leaned forward and the doctor crouched into an awkward sumo wrestler position. A glob of my come dripped from her pussy and landed on the floor. Eve begged to be fucked harder. The doctor spread Adam's hairy ass cheeks. She spat on her hand a couple of times and slathered the saliva on the dildo before easing it into Adam's ass. The doctor fucked Adam and he tried to match her rhythm to fuck Eve. The two of them fucking in one even thrust looked like a grotesque dance. Eve and Adam both moaned in ecstasy as the doctor controlled the force and rhythm of their intercourse.

Dr. Paxter said, "Yeah. You like me fucking you, don't you? You want our lord's cock inside your filthy anus. You're a despicable man and unworthy of his seed."

"Oh yes," Adam panted. "I want his cock inside me. I want to pleasure the lord the way he has allowed for me to be pleasured. Fuck me hard!"

I bucked wildly. My struggle caused the cart to hop off the ground. The room was filled with the sweet smell of pussy and the cloying stench of Adam's ass. The trio ignored me and continued their orgy. I tried to either loosen the ropes by pulling on them or wiggling my arms through them. The result was more pain and black dots swimming in my vision. Adam cried out, signaling his orgasm, and slammed his hips into Eve a couple more times.

Dr. Paxter withdrew the dildo from Adam's ass and stood. Adam panted as he regained himself. While still on his knees he turned to face the doctor. Eve sat back on her haunches and began to masturbate. Adam's semen slid from Eve's vagina and pooled on the floor, connected by a thin line. The doctor grabbed the base of the now shit covered dildo and pointed it toward Adam's face.

I groaned. "Please don't."

Adam eagerly took the dildo in his mouth. I retched. The doctor placed her hand on the back of Adam's head and forced the dildo further into his mouth until he gagged. I barely had time to turn my head to the side before I vomited what bile I had in my stomach.

Eve rose and approached me. A long string of Adam's come seeped from her cunt.

"Get away from me!" I yelled. I spat the remaining debris of vomit at her but missed.

Eve laughed at my failed attempt to insult her and straddled me. I looked down at my cock and panicked. I was covered in the doctor's come and still erect. I thrust my weight backward trying to move away from Eve and slammed my hip into the railing of the cart. The searing pain in my arms forced me to stop. Come dripped from Eve's vagina and onto my stomach.

"Don't get near me you filthy whore!" I looked at my penis. "I don't want to fuck you, skank." I wailed like a wounded animal as the come she dripped on my stomach slid down the side of my belly.

Adam gagged again as the doctor rammed the dildo into his mouth. The doctor laughed at him and egged him to suck the lord off.

Eve knelt down but didn't take my penis inside her. "Relax," she said. "It's not that bad. Besides, you'll get to fuck Elizabeth and Lauren and the other girls from town."

I whimpered something unintelligible but she cut me off.

"You don't have to do anything," Eve said. "The doctor will keep you medicated so you're always hard. All you have to do is fuck us."

The doctor finished fucking Adam's mouth and slapped the side of his face softly with the soiled phallus. The two laughed and playfully taunted each other.

When they were done horsing around Adam stood and said, "It's a guy's dream come true. Fuck who and when you want."

I said, "You're warped."

The doctor sighed. "If you continue to complain and be negative I'll gag you and never untie you." She waved her strap on at me menacingly and smirked. "Now . . . you can either do what you're told and make it easy on all of us or—"

"Fuck you!" I spat. "You cut off my fucking thumbs! You're all a bunch of psychopaths! There is no *or*. I'm not going to be a part of your fucked up fetish. Untie me and get the fuck out of my house!" I nodded toward Eve. "And take the whore with you. None of you are welcome here."

The three of them laughed at me. The doctor doubled over with humor and Adam laughed so hard his eyes watered. Eve took my penis and guided it inside of her. I closed my eyes and tried to block the others out but they continued to laugh as Eve fucked me. I came again without warning and the orgasm was strong. The trio stopped mocking me when I groaned in ecstasy. The orgasm caused my stomach to sink as if I was on a rollercoaster. The duration between start and finish was shorter than before. I didn't know what kind of drug they'd given me to make that possible. I hadn't bounced back quickly after ejaculating since I was a teenager. I opened my eyes as Eve rose off me. My come dribbled out of her as she stepped over me.

Eve walked over to a wall. She placed both hands on the wall, arched her back, and spread her legs. The doctor approached her, grabbed the strap on, and eased it into Eve's ass. Dr. Paxter gripped Eve's hips and proceeded to fuck her.

Adam watched them with a hard on and fondled his testicles. I cursed at them. The girls ignored me and continued their sex act. Eve begged the doctor to rail her ass until she bled. Adam looked at me and cupped his balls. I spit at him. My saliva landed on the floor. He looked at me incredulously and dropped his hand from his nuts. He pursed his lips and walked behind the cart where I couldn't see him.

A moment later his dumb face hovered above my head. He forced a ball gag into my mouth. I tried to bite him but the gag made it impossible. I clenched my jaw tight but he wrapped the straps around my head and cinched them, causing the ball to be forced deeper into my mouth. I was afraid he'd break my teeth. The strap pulled my hair and ripped strands of it out.

Adam lifted the hand truck and wheeled me into the hall. The girls either didn't notice or care Adam was moving me.

We were at the end of the hall on the first floor. I could detect the edge of the mirror on the door leading to the house down the hallway. With all the commotion in the room I hadn't noticed how much noise was coming from the other rooms. A cacophony of sex resounded from everywhere.

Adam wheeled me down the hall. We passed the first door and inside Lauren was eating out the masculine woman from the gas station. At the next door I spotted a greasy-haired teen boy fucking the surly nurse from Dr. Paxter's office in the ass.

I'd never seen the kid before. And I didn't have to look to know the kid was thumbless. This was the reason I hadn't met another male in town other than Adam. Every man had the same affliction and it would've been a major red flag something was wrong.

I shut my eyes and silently begged some unknown deity for help. I didn't want to see anymore. And the best I could do was wish I could somehow escape or someone would send the cops to check on me when I hadn't responded to any work emails or phone calls after a few days. But who knew what would happen until then. I could be dead before anyone thought something was wrong.

Adam wheeled me down the hall and I felt sick to my stomach again. I didn't think there was anything left to vomit, but if there was, I might drown in my own bile with the gag in. I felt the inertia of the cart turn and thought I might fall over. The cart was sat in a standing position this time. I opened my eyes and found myself in one of the empty rooms. There were no other couples fucking. It was just me and Adam.

Adam left the room and I breathed a small sigh of relief. I didn't dare move in fear the cart would topple over. I didn't think I could bear much more physical pain since my hands had taken to throbbing.

I listened to the various sex acts taking place in the other rooms. After a few minutes Adam reappeared with a cinderblock. I panicked as I realized how vulnerable I was and Adam had an unconventional weapon. I tried to plead around the gag. He ignored me and went about his task.

He sat the concrete block on the floor a few feet in front of me and walked behind the cart. I sensed him taking the handles right before the cart began to tip forward. I threw my weight backward but Adam held tight and continued to lower me toward the floor.

"Don't flop like a fish," he said. "I'm liable to drop you on your face."

He lowered me until my chest was on the block. The platform of the cart kept my toes from being smashed into the ground. But my weight caused the concrete to scratch and bite my skin. My backside was exposed between the two bars of the cart.

Adam's foot smacked the ground when he straddled the cart. A fear I'd never experienced before gripped my gut when his fingers probed my ass crack. I thrashed and clenched my buttocks, trapping Adam's fingers between my cheeks. He wiggled his fingers and I felt as if I were being probed by stone worms. He began to insert one of his digits into my anus. My screams were pitiful sounding around the gag. Slobber dripped from my mouth and onto the floor as I howled. The cinderblock cut my skin as I struggled and the cuts stung.

A burning sensation began in my anus as he pushed his fingers deeper inside me. I feared he was doing irreparable damage to my insides. I tried to rock the cart from side to side to knock him down but Adam outweighed me considerably. He pinched the cart between his legs and laid a forearm on my back, holding me down. His weight made it difficult to breathe and the concrete block cut deeper into my chest. He slid his finger in and out of my ass like a tiny articulated penis.

"You're tight," he whispered in my ear. "Like you've never been fucked in the ass before."

I begged him to stop. He grunted and groaned with satisfaction in my ear. My muffled pleas began to work. He withdrew his finger. But he didn't move and the relief only lasted a heartbeat. He spat on his hand beside my face and slathered my anus with the secretion. I clenched my buttocks again. He spat a second time and I knew he was coating his penis. I screamed so hard I began to choke and cough.

Adam leaned most of his weight on his arm to hold me still. I struggled to keep breathing. He began to force his dick in my ass. A fiery pain I'd never experienced before—even after a day of extreme diarrhea—sored through my asshole as he entered and tore the tender skin.

I screamed and screamed and screamed and choked and coughed as he fucked me. My ass was on fire and I was sure when this was done he would stand the cart up and my insides would fall on the ground. I was being disemboweled through my anus.

He breathed in my ear. "Relax and it won't hurt so bad."

His pace quickened and he began to grunt when he thrust. His fat stomach slapped the top of my ass as he worked. I gagged. The pain was unbearable and after a few minutes his thrusts were accompanied by wet smacking noises. I was humiliated and infuriated and everything was surreal and I was helpless to do anything to stop my violation. I didn't want to relax because that was giving up. But I knew he was right. The less I fought the less damage and pain there would be when it was over.

I refused to give in. I focused on the pool of saliva on the floor I had produced from screaming. I tried to block out what was happening but the pain in my anus made it impossible. I redirected my thoughts to the pain in my hands. Something tapped my back a few times before I realized Adam was dripping sweat on me. He began to hump more forcefully. The pain in my ass intensified. He gave one final thrust and called out in bliss. He was still for a few seconds. Once he finally caught his breath he withdrew his penis. But the searing pain in my anus didn't subside. It felt like my asshole was dilated and would never return to its normal size.

Adam stepped over me and stood by my head. His feet were veiny and his toenails were thick and yellow. He lifted the cart back into a standing position. Blood trickled down my chest from the deep scratches caused by the cinderblock. Something ran down the inside of my thigh. I thought it might be sweat until I noticed the blood and shit caking Adam's still erect penis. The room was acrid with sweat and shit and come and blood and somewhere it smelled like someone was spinning cotton candy and doing something with roses and it made my nostrils and throat burn.

The doctor called for Adam in a singsong voice from somewhere down the hall.

"In here," he answered.

He stroked his filthy penis the best he could without the help of his missing digit. I focused on the fingers I had left and tried to move them. I winced at the pain and tried to ignore Adam as he clumsily masturbated. A half a minute passed before the doctor entered the room. Adam was still attempting to masturbate.

"There you are," she said.

The doctor still wore the strap on. She gave Adam a disapproving look when she realized what he was doing and crossed her arms. Adam let go of his cock, shrugged, and lift-

KITUALISTIC HUMAN SACRIFICE

ed his foul hands in surrender. His face reddened. Dr. Paxter glanced at his soiled hands and then to me. She took in my demeanor, the cuts on my chest, the cinderblock, and Adam who now stared at the floor like a dog who knew it was in trouble.

Anger washed over the doctor's features. She stomped toward Adam. He lifted his hands to shield his face as the doctor swung one arm back. She held her arm in a strike position and grabbed Adam's arm with her other hand. She spun him around and firmly planted a slap on his buttocks.

She reprimanded him and spanked him again. "How many times do I have to tell you? Your seed is for the lord!"

He squealed. "I'm sorry! I'm sorry!"

The doctor stopped the discipline. She stepped back from him and massaged her reddened hand. She said, "Take him to the circle. It's time for the sacrifices."

I screamed and they both turned to me with confused expressions as if they'd forgotten I was in the room. I begged the doctor not to kill me. It took a couple of times of repeating the phrase with the gag before she understood me.

She laughed as I pleaded for my life. "Don't worry. You're not innocent enough to give to the lord."

She exited the room with a smile. Adam and I were alone again.

17

Adam wheeled me toward the mirrored door. He sat the cart in the upright position and I was faced with my reflection. I could see dried blood and shit on the inside of my thigh. Adam reveled in my self-inspection over my shoulder. He reached between my ass cheeks and inserted his finger in my anus. I flinched as the searing pain was renewed. I didn't have the energy to scream any more. Adam fingered my ass for a few seconds before he stepped around the cart to face me. He pointed the finger he'd had in me at my chest. The digit was now covered in blood and shit and come. He began to draw something on my chest in the foul mixture. The stench was awful and I turned my head to avoid it. I'd never thought about murdering anyone in my entire life but at that moment I'd reached a breaking point. This new anger calmed me and cleared my head.

Adam stepped to the side and stared into the mirror to admire his artwork and my reaction to his creation. He'd drawn an upside down pentagram on my chest. My expression was vacant.

"Leave your soul here," he said. "You're not gonna need it anymore."

He laughed, opened the door, and wheeled me into the living room. An enthusiastic couple I'd never seen before followed us. A few seconds later Lauren and the nurse and the greasy-haired teen arrived. They took it upon themselves to seat their filthy naked bodies on my sofa. More and more people filed into the room. All of them were covered in varying degrees of sweat and shit and come and blood and the living room smelled like a truck stop gloryhole. Some took it upon themselves to fill the time by fucking on my furniture. I knew the second I was free I had to burn the house to the ground—not caring if Eve was inside—and never come back.

A naked redheaded woman clearly classified as morbidly obese waddled into the room. She huffed with each step she took. Her pale and veiny skin was covered in a sheen of sweat. Stretchmarks covered her flabby upper arms, sagging breasts, the hanging stomach covering her sex, and her bulging and cellulite dimpled thighs. She squealed when she spotted me and clapped her meaty hands. She thundered over to me excitedly and told Adam to set the cart down. I moaned when he did what she told him and wished they'd cut off my dick instead of my thumbs.

The massive woman stepped over the cart like a sumo wrestler. Her stomach shifted as she did so and I got a glimpse of her cavernous and hairy vagina below her stomach. I dry heaved when a loogie of come dropped out of her and landed on my dick. She took Adam's dick in her mouth and grabbed my never ending erection. She shifted her belly and guided my dick inside her. I tried to wiggle away from her but she crushed me into the metal frame of the cart each time she humped me. I could feel another bruise forming each time she dropped her massive weight on me. Her large thighs slapped my wounded hands and I bit the gag to keep from screaming. I focused on some of the others in the room having sex. There was nothing arousing about what was happening to me but I was helpless to control my body. All I knew was that I wanted it to be over. It didn't take long. My body tensed when it happened and I barked with the release. The woman kept fucking me and sucking Adam's cock. When my orgasm subsided I tried to tell her to stop.

She stopped sucking Adam, continued to fuck me, and

said, "What?"

I said I was done. She stared down at me, confused, and the intensity of her humping began to waver. I cringed when she came to a complete stop. Her heavy thighs rested on my hands and pinned them against the cart. She looked to Adam. He shrugged. Adam reached behind my head and unbuckled the gag. He pulled the contraption from my mouth and let it fall to the floor.

I adjusted my sore jaw and stretched my stiff neck. I said, "I'm done."

The redhead said, "Oh."

The relief I felt when she stepped over me was better than any orgasm I'd ever had. She casually flopped down on the chaise lounge and began looking for another partner. Adam lifted my cart back to the standing position. Dr. Paxter entered the room.

The living room was now filled with a motley crew. There were a handful of men but the group was mainly composed of women. Some of the girls didn't look old enough to be legal. All of them were naked with the exception of the doctor and her strap on and she now carried a black leather backpack. The few people who were still fucking stopped when the doctor appeared.

"All right, children," the doctor said. "Let's not leave Nana Mary waiting."

The doctor's statement prompted the group to file out of the house in a leisurely and orderly fashion as if it were a normal gathering. One woman complimented another on her new hairstyle. I overheard a man ask another if he ever fixed his lawn mower. The sheer casualness of the crowd was baffling. Adam turned the cart toward the door. I spotted my gag on the floor and hoped no one else would. I thanked the powers that be for Adam's absentmindedness as he steered me out the front door.

The night air was freezing. The moon was full and the sky contained a few wispy clouds. The effect was striking. The moon acted as a dim sun with the absence of light pollution.

The group of people walked, pranced, and jogged naked through the night toward the trees at the back of the property. Their bodies cast shadows on the grayed night grass and the moonlight highlighted their naked flesh. The moon illuminated a snake of smoke above the tree line. A faint odor of campfire and burning leaves haunted the air.

Adam was a well of strength and energy. He maneuvered the cart across the dewy grass without any difficulty. Once the group was at the trailhead the doctor removed a few flashlights from her bag and passed them around. She kept one for herself.

Lauren took one of the flashlights, turned it on, and disappeared down the trail. The others continued their banal chatter and followed her. They whooped and laughed and carried on into the dark woods. Beams of broken light bounced through the dense trees.

Eventually the only people left were me, Adam, and the doctor. Dr. Paxter took up the tail and lit the way for us. Adam carefully pushed me down the path so I could see where we were headed.

"Where are we going?" I said.

The doctor snapped, "I thought you gagged him!"

"Shit," Adam said. "I took it off 'cause he was addressin' Miss Nancy." He stopped. "I can go back—"

"We don't have time," she said. She stopped abruptly, spun, and shone the light in Adam's face. "It'll be your fault if he's disruptive." She redirected the light to my face. "I have the tools to cut off your tongue if you ruin this. And I won't sedate you for the procedure."

I was blinded by her light and shut my eyes tight. She smacked one of my bandaged hands. I held back a scream when the pain renewed. As much as I wanted to spit in her face I decided my best strategy was to keep quiet at this point. I would let them do what they wanted as long as it didn't cause me any more pain. An even better plan was to pretend I *wanted* to be a part of whatever insane thing they were doing. Maybe someone would untie me if they thought I would participate willingly. Once I was free I would make a run for it and get the fuck out of this town. Because deep down I knew everyone in the town was a part of the sex cult . . . most likely even the police.

She didn't drop the light from my face.

I said, "I won't be a disruption. I just wanna know what's going on. I don't like surprises."

She pointed the light at the ground. I opened my eyes but they had some difficulty readjusting to the scantily lit night. The doctor redirected the flashlight below her chin and the affect cast eerie shadows across her face. If I didn't already have goosebumps from cold fall air I was certain the shadows of her expression would have raised them. She smiled and the lighting made her appear malevolent. She waved the light to insinuate Adam should follow and she proceeded down the path. We continued in silence. I considered asking again where we were going or what we were doing but honestly I didn't want to know. I knew wherever we were going and whatever we were doing was not good. The doctor's threat of cutting out my tongue kept me quiet.

I thought about how the doc mentioned sacrifices. And then I thought about their macabre orgy. Why did they need me? The doctor said they wouldn't sacrifice me. But amputating my thumbs was not a blasé move and all of them seemed to think it was. There was no way I could trust anything any of them said. They were going to kill me regardless of what they told me. What good was I to them alive? I began to panic and hyperventilate.

The doctor sighed and said, "What is it now?"

She did not stop or slow down or bother to turn to me when she spoke. Getting to the destination was her priority.

"I don't want to be sacrificed!" I blurted.

I refused to bawl and kept breathing erratically. There was no way I would let these psychos have the satisfaction of making me cry. It was bad enough I was *begging* for my life. The crux of the situation was I didn't think I could've cried if I wanted to.

The two laughed at me but didn't let the caravan slow. The procession continued down the trail without as much as a hiccup.

"You're not worthy to sacrifice," the doctor said.

Adam mocked me. I wanted to scream I didn't trust them and needed some sort of assurance beyond their words that I wouldn't die tonight without a way to defend myself.

A mass uniform chanting ahead on the path caught my attention and a large flickering light bled through the dense foliage. The trees on the path started to close in and I knew we were close to the clearing I'd found before. Adam turned the cart and pulled me over some fallen logs. Dr. Paxter helped to lift the cart over an especially large trunk. The odor of the bonfire was strong. Singing and chanting and sounds of laughter filled the night.

Adam continued to pull me down the path. I couldn't see what we were entering any longer. My view was of the reflecting firelight on the trees and darkness of the unlit path behind us. A few tree branches scraped the naked skin of my arms and legs as we moved down the narrowing path. Before I knew it we were in the clearing. Adam turned the cart so I faced the ensuing chaos. Couples fucked on the ground and on the benches positioned on either side of the fire. People danced erratically and sang. A few of the group's members cheered when they noticed we'd arrived.

Among the havoc one figure stood out more than any other. While the others worked themselves into a frenzy, Nana Mary stood motionless by the fire. She wore a black hooded cloak. The garment was open in the front to expose her paper thin skin hanging loosely over her time twisted body. Her sagging breasts hung to her navel and her large dark nipples pointed at the ground. The withered inner lips of her dried and useless cunt protruded excessively beyond a massive grayed bush. She held a book in the crook of her arm and stared vacantly into the fire. The flames reflected on the lenses of her glasses. The image of her motionlessness and the dancing flames in her vision, along with the disorder around her, brought on a fear greater than any other I'd experienced. My bowels felt loose.

The doctor called the group to attention. "All right, children! It's time for the ceremony to begin!"

Couples stopped their intercourse in mid thrust. Everyone moved nonchalantly to their predetermined positions. The men retreated to the edges of the clearing. Adam moved my cart so I completed the large circle the men were forming. I had a clear view of what was taking place at the center near the fire. Adam stood beside me as the events unfolded. The women circled the fire and left a small berth for Nana Mary who stood in the same stance as before.

Dr. Paxter pulled the backpack off her back and held it by the strap. She unzipped the bag and proceeded around the circle of women. She took an item from within the bag and handed it to each woman. Once she made it around the circle she retrieved one for herself, along with a secondary item, and sat the bag on the ground.

I whispered, "What are they doing?"

Adam reprimanded me with a quiet shush.

The doctor said, "Daughters." She held up one of the items.

The women took the item in both hands and appeared to pop the top off. Some of the women squatted and held the object between their legs. Others stood bowlegged. A few of them began to urinate freely. It took a few seconds for it to dawn on me they were taking pregnancy tests. The doctor was the first one finished. She replaced the cap on the testing stick and waited patiently for the others to do the same. She glanced at the other item she held—a cellphone. She thumbed a few commands and began timing the mass test. A few of the women talked quietly amongst themselves. The timer sounded and the doctor told them to check their tests. The women held their sticks to the firelight to read the results. The ones whose tests were positive gave cheers as if they'd won a prize and stood next to Nana Mary. The whole scene reminded me of a demented version of *The Price is Right*. Nana Mary made a terrible gameshow host. She was indifferent to everything. And I wished she would close the cloak over her time ravaged body.

Once the women determined who was pregnant and who wasn't, the ones who were unfertilized joined the men at the outskirts. In the end seven women received a positive test result. One was Lauren and another was the fat redheaded cow Adam called Nancy. Three of the fertile women I'd never seen before and the last I recognized half hidden by the group was Eve.

I felt as if I'd been dropped from a skyscraper. Rage flooded through me. The cunt was pregnant with someone else's child.

I couldn't help myself. I yelled, "Slut!"

Everyone grew quiet and looked at me except Nana Mary who stood unflinching. The firelight cast dancing shadows across everyone's features. The group should've appeared intimidating but I was too furious to care. I was positive Eve smirked which made me even more angry. Eve had skyrocketed to the top of my list of people to murder when given the chance.

The doctor pointed at me. "Nick," she said in a singsong voice. "What did I tell you?" She extended her tongue and drew an imaginary line across it with her finger.

My body was tense. I tried to relax. I clenched my jaw and nodded at Dr. Paxter. The doctor turned back to the group and directed the pregnant women to the benches on either side of the fire. Lauren and Eve and two teenage girls stood facing the bench closest to me which gave me a view of their backsides. Lauren appeared to have an ample amount of feces smeared on her ass from being butt fucked. The other three women took up the other bench, including the obese woman. The doctor rummaged in her bag and withdrew a wire coat hanger.

My body went numb when I realized what was going to happen. I was certain my brain broke at that very moment. I felt disconnected from my body and every ounce of my inner self flew into a frenzy but physically I felt dead. I could only stare at the events unfolding.

Lauren was up first. She bent over the bench by the fire. The doctor bent the hanger into a flat oblong loop, using the hook as a handle. She held the weapon with one hand and inserted the strap on dildo into Lauren's pussy and began to fuck her.

Nana Mary opened the book she held. I recognized its unusual appearance as one from Dr. Paxter's shelf. Mary read from it as the doctor fucked the girl. "He comes to inseminate the world with his seed so he shall be born amongst men. He will rule the crafted men of God and allow them to use their gift of creation as they see fit."

The doctor removed the false phallus from Lauren. She laid the hanger on Lauren's lower back and spread her buttocks to open her cunt. Dr. Paxter shaped her fingers into a cone and inserted them into Lauren's vagina. She worked her hand in and out of the girl's pussy until she was able to insert her whole hand. Lauren called out in ecstasy as the doctor fisted her.

Nana Mary bellowed, "Without rules! Without repercussions! We will live of our own free will without our creator! The castoff has promised us a life without sin!"

The doctor removed her hand from Lauren, took up the hanger, and knelt behind her. The doctor held the hooked end of the coat hanger and inserted the looped end into Lauren's pussy. It only went in to a certain point and appeared to meet an obstruction. The doctor braced her smegma-covered hand on Lauren's ass and forced the hanger in. Lauren screamed when the tool suddenly slipped deeper inside her vagina. The doctor wiggled the device around in a circular motion several times. Lauren screamed the entire time until the doctor removed the hanger. Blood flowed from the girl's pussy and down her leg as soon as the hanger was removed. Lauren wept and rested her weight over the bench. The muscles on the back of the girl's thighs twitched. The doctor stood.

Nana Mary raised the hand not holding the tome and proclaimed, "He must be conceived six hundred and sixty-five times before his final birth! This daughter has given the three hundred seventy-second! Praise the mother of our lord!"

The group said in unison, "Praise Lauren!"

Lauren continued to cry softly. The doctor moved to the next woman, Eve. Without ceremony Dr. Paxter began to fuck Eve. Nana Mary repeated the same phrases she had with Lauren's procedure.

The shock of what was happening wore off. I felt sick. A large part of me enjoyed watching Eve being fisted. I wanted to shout triumphantly when the doctor inserted the hanger into Eve's cunt. I enjoyed watching her have an abortion preformed in the most unsanitary environment. The doctor hadn't bothered to wash anything between the procedures and used the exact same hanger. I wished Eve would've been last in the lineup. I wanted all of the blood and shit and old come to accumulate on the dildo and hanger before entering her. I relished in her agony when the hanger was fully inserted. My cock hardened to the point of pain when she began to cry. A part of me would've loved to hate fuck her in the ass while the doctor aborted whoever's child she was pregnant with.

Nana Mary proclaimed the ceremony was the three hundred and seventy-third. Everyone praised Eve and the doctor moved on to the next girl. Eve continued to lean over the bench with Lauren and the two wept and bled.

The doctor worked her way through the women. There was no deviation in the ceremony. All of the women continued to stay in their positions after their abortion was complete.

Nancy moaned like a cow during her abortion and was the only one who didn't cry. She appeared to enjoy the pain she was in. The last girl in the lineup was fresh-faced and had tiny lumps for breasts. She barely looked thirteen years old and I dry heaved when the doctor fist fucked her.

When the doctor was finished she stood beside Nana Mary. The men on the outskirts approached the bleeding and sobbing women. My eyes burned from the smoke and I wasn't sure if I'd blinked since the ceremony had started. All of this was wrong. It was sick. But I couldn't take my eyes off the tragedy unraveling before me. I was engrossed in the commotion and didn't realize Adam had stepped behind me. The cart began to lean back and my body jerked with a start. I thought I'd done something to cause the cart to fall backward. I pulled my hands against their bindings to catch myself and winced at the renewed pain.

Adam wheeled me toward the group assembled around the fire. He sat the cart behind Eve. I fixated on the blood running down her inner thigh. She looked over her shoulder at me. She'd stopped crying and looked at me indifferently. I knew we were both lost to the other forever. There was no return. There was no fixing us. There hadn't been for a very long time. We'd been two people going through the actions of living and loving one another but the inflection of our joined existence was snuffed out so long ago neither of us could tell you when it had happened. I couldn't remember the last time I felt anything for her but hate or annoyance. If the circumstances of the current events were removed I would feel no different. I couldn't help but feel sorry for her for being weak and not walking away. Instead she stubbornly tried to manipulate a catastrophe into something she wanted. And regardless if she succeeded or failed she wore a smile and told herself, and the world, the result was what she'd intended and wanted the entire time. Because she couldn't admit she'd failed.

The doctor left Nana Mary's side and approached me. She held the bloodied coat hanger. Adam went to stand behind the redheaded woman.

Nana Mary said, "We've succeeded three hundred seventy-eight times! The mothers of our lord must be christened once again with his seed!"

The men stepped up to the women and began to fuck them. Some of the woman cooed. Others were silent. The girl who'd received the last abortion cried as a gross greasy-haired teen fucked her gleefully. Eve was the only one who didn't have a partner.

The doctor said, "We figured it might be easier for you if you inseminated Eve."

The greasy-haired teen came in no time and gasped in ecstasy. The sobbing girl below him had to be thrilled it was over. He removed his bloody cock from her and retreated to the edge of the clearing.

I looked at Eve's bleeding cunt and at the expectant doctor. I wasn't sure what kind of response she was waiting for but I burst into uncontrollable laughter. My reaction angered the doctor. None of the others flinched. They continued their mission. My outburst was insignificant to the importance of their orgy and they all carried on as if I wasn't there. The laughter turned into a nonstop chortle and the doctor slapped me. I stopped.

"I'll cut out your fucking tongue," she said. "We're giving you an opportunity to be a part of something your insignificant brain can't begin to understand. You could be the father of our lord! Your name would be written into history books."

I was physically and mentally exhausted. The surreal events had worn me down and desensitized me. I was slaphappy. My amusement raged back when she told me I could be a father. I laughed hard and couldn't catch my breath. Without warning the doctor whipped my testicles with the fouled hanger. I screamed with what little air remained in my lungs. The pain made me nauseous and I began to sweat. I tried to cross my bound legs and double over but the rope was unrelenting. The cold night air, combined with my sweat, made me shiver.

"Stop laughing!" the doctor yelled.

Some of the men stopped fucking the women. The few who continued slowed their pace and focused their attention on me. Nana Mary shut the book she held and gave me a disapproving look.

The doctor said, "There is nothing funny about this." She pointed the disgusting hanger in my face. "I'm going to untie you and you're going to fuck your wife." She poked the pentagram on my chest with the hanger. "You will fuck her whenever she wants. You will also fuck the other women in town when they want. And you will participate and rejoice at the ceremonies when there has been conception and not make a mockery of it."

"Conception?" I laughed. "There won't be any conception."

Everyone came to a complete standstill. All eyes were on me, expectantly waiting for me to clarify.

I said, "I've had a vasectomy. I can't get anyone pregnant unless it's immaculate conception." I laughed.

Whispers and murmuring erupted amongst the group. Eve stood and turned to face me. The doctor looked to Nana Mary for an answer.

Eve said to the doctor, "He didn't have a vasectomy. He's lying."

"I'm not lying," I said to Eve. "I did it since you got pregnant behind my back. You didn't ask me for permission so I didn't need yours. I couldn't trust you wouldn't get knocked up again after you had the first one."

The group grew quiet. Everyone looked to Nana Mary for answers to an unspoken question. The only sound was the crackle of the fire.

Nana Mary said, "Take him to the church."

The doctor snapped her fingers at Adam. She also beckoned the greasy-haired teen forward. Adam tilted the cart and began to pull it toward the path.

"What are you going to do?" I shouted.

No one answered. I screamed and demanded an answer. When no one acknowledged me I begged to be let go. Pleading was unfruitful and I tried bargaining. I told them I would leave town and never tell a soul about this place. I told them they could have the house.

The group started their orgy again as we slowly crossed the clearing. The women who'd stood around the edge joined the others by the fire. Some of them began to eat the pussies of the newly aborted women while others fucked and sucked the men. The throng became a wriggling mass of flesh and blood and fucking and moans and shadows as the fire flickered out of sync with their movements.

I demanded to be untied. Right before we started down the path the doctor broke away from the orgy and called for us to stop. Adam set the cart down as Dr. Paxter disappeared into the swarm of flesh and reappeared holding a small object. She headed toward us in a hurry. I hoped she was bringing a tool to cut the ropes but something told me it was something more sinister. I clenched my jaw and relished the last few seconds of having my tongue intact.

The doctor stopped in front of me and popped the safety cap off a syringe. She stabbed my arm and injected me before I had time to protest. My tongue became thick instantly. I tried to tell her I would disappear and no one would ever see me again but my words came out garbled.

The orgy became a whirlpool of colors and sounds and smells. I thought I spotted a large shadowy figure standing in the middle of the group. Someone called out in ecstasy but the sound wasn't human. The group appeared animalistic and predatory.

Dr. Paxter strolled back to the ceremony. Eve was on all fours on the ground, facing my direction. She watched me with a nonchalant expression while a large man gripped her hair and fucked her savagely from behind.

The drug the doctor injected me with overtook me and I entered the abyss of sleep.

18

My head throbbed and my skull felt three times bigger than the skin covering it. There was an overwhelming sensation of falling as I regained consciousness. The air was thick and smelled of something rotten. A low buzzing filled my ears and I wasn't sure if they were ringing from the pressure in my head or some external noise. It took some time for me to make sense of where I was and the state I was in.

I hung upside down and tied to an inverted cross at the head of what appeared to be a pulpit in a church. The ropes binding my arms were cautious of my bandaged hands but the ones around my ankles were too tight and my feet were bloodless and asleep. The cross was suspended a few feet from the ground and a large square altar was located in front of me. Angry flies buzzed around a pile of gory offal covering the altar. I tried to display my disgust but found I'd been gagged again.

I was surrounded by red candles and the light quality was poor.

The drug I was injected with made it difficult to focus. As my vision adjusted to the light I found I wasn't alone. The congregation slowly became recognizable. Once their demeanor and dress was distinguishable I began to panic and the adrenaline cleared the drug-induced fogginess from my head.

The pews were filled with naked people wearing goat masks. The masks had nubby horns and were realistic in shape, size, and quality. They looked to be fashioned from actual taxidermy goats. The people were silent and motionless. I recognized Eve's and Lauren's nude bodies in the front row. The people in the pews were the same people from the orgy.

Two figures appeared from either side of the stage and approached the altar. I knew the one wearing the unmistakable strap on was Dr. Paxter. The other was stooped and cloaked—Nana Mary. The two also wore masks but theirs were different than the congregation's. Dr. Paxter's was adorned with two large sets of elaborate horns while Nana Mary's was dyed or painted bright red. They stopped in front of the altar and faced the people seated in the pews.

Nana Mary unfastened her cloak and let it fall to the ground. Even in the terrible lighting I could discern the hideous effects of age in her deteriorating body: sagging skin, broken veins, and stretchmarks. She raised her arms and began to speak in a language I didn't know. Her affliction sounded passionate and frenzied. The doctor stood motionless beside her as she continued to preach to the crowd. Nana Mary paused briefly.

The people responded with a short simultaneous chant, "We beg of our lord to incarnate in the flesh of our mother, Elizabeth."

Nana Mary and the doctor faced each other. Nana Mary laid her arthritic hands on Dr. Paxter's breasts, tilted her face toward the ceiling, and began to moan.

The congregation chanted, "Copulate with the crone in ceremony for she is barren and only gives birth to pleasure."

The doctor growled and her whole body tensed. She grabbed the old woman's arms and thrust her toward the altar. Nana Mary's torso landed on the foul viscera with a wet smack. Some of the unidentifiable tissue slid across the altar toward me and the flies took flight. I flinched as some of the gore fell on the ground and something splattered on my face and neck. The old woman yelped in pain and the doctor was on top of her in a flash. Nana Mary's arms slipped through the entrails as Dr. Paxter bent her over the table and began to fuck her with the strap on. Nana Mary moaned and Dr. Paxter pushed the woman's masked face into the repugnant material covering the altar. The candlelight danced across the shiny substance and it appeared alive and wriggling. I thought the light was playing tricks on my eyes until I noticed the maggots. I gagged. The doctor looked up at me as she fucked Nana Mary. I couldn't see her eyes behind the mask in the faint light but I knew we were making eye contact. Until then I thought she might have assumed I was still unconscious.

The old woman moaned again. She sounded like she was in pain. It was hard to tell with her masked face smashed into the maggot mess.

The doctor stepped back and pushed Nana Mary roughly onto the altar. The old woman slid across the surface, knocking most of the viscera to the floor. She almost fell off the other side but caught herself. The doctor instructed her to get on all fours and joined her on top of the altar. Dr. Paxter kneeled behind Nana Mary, grabbed a handful of the viscera, and crassly began to stuff it into the old woman's cunt. She added a couple more handfuls before she started fisting Nana Mary's anus. Nana Mary began to sob and wail.

I wanted to close my eyes to all of it but the unreality of it forced me to watch. I wanted to wake up. I wanted to roll over in my apartment with Eve by my side and find it was all a terrible dream. Eve had never been pregnant. We had never moved. These people didn't exist. This wasn't happening. I'd watched one too many fucked up pornos and this was what my sick, fucked up imagination concocted in my sleep. I sought out Eve in the front row. She watched the scene like the others—unmoving and unflinching.

The doctor slid her fist into the old woman a few more times before she finally removed her hand from Nana Mary's ass. The old woman splayed her arms and legs across the altar and let herself lie flat on her stomach. She pressed her mask into the maggot infested meat and sobbed. The doctor slipped off the altar and rubbed the feces and blood and gore from her hands over her breasts in a sensual manner. The crowd watched in silence.

The doctor raised her arms and yelled, "I am your lord and I'm pleasured by your offering!" She reached in between her legs and began to finger her cunt.

The group cheered. The doctor spun to face me and masturbated. The congregation continued to cheer and a few rose to their feet. The doctor's chest heaved from her exertions and she threw her head back and cried out in ecstasy. The motion of her hand slowed and she started toward me. The people in the pews became frenzied. Some of the followers jumped up and down excitedly as the doctor approached me. She dropped her hand from her pussy.

I was suspended far enough from the ground that my face was the same height as the doctor's. I couldn't see her actual eyes, only the reflection of the dim candlelight off the wet surface of them. The stench of her was awful and I dry heaved. I could feel the burn of bile in the back of my throat. The doctor grabbed my face with the hand she'd inserted into Nana Mary's ass. I tried to jerk away from her but my motions were limited. She laughed and forced me to look at her.

The slimy texture of the filth on her hands made my spine scream with revulsion. She laughed and rubbed both of her hands over my face. I screamed and pulled on the unforgiving restraints. A couple of stitches in my right hand tore through the skin. I screamed again. The doctor stopped grinding her hands on me and turned to face the audience. I gagged hard and broke wind.

The doctor bellowed at the group. "Shut up!"

The crowd quieted. Even Nana Mary stopped sobbing.

The doctor approached the altar and took up handfuls of the viscera and squeezed it. She appeared to be questioning the dripping gore in her hands. "What would you have me do with the barren man?"

Nana Mary whimpered. The doctor threw the viscera at her masked face. The old woman flinched.

Nana Mary said, "We offer him as a sacrifice since he cannot take part in the prophecy?" The statement sounded more like a question.

I screamed and thrashed and hoped I could somehow topple the cross. The townspeople erupted into cheers.

I noticed a shadow step into the aisle near the doors at the back of the church. It was hard to discern but they appeared clothed or possibly wearing robes like Nana Mary's. The figure raised one arm and discharged a firearm at the ceiling. The noise was tremendous and the congregation cowered in the pews. Nana Mary threw her arms over her head to shield herself from harm. The doctor didn't flinch. The person trained the gun on the doctor and strode casually down the aisle.

"That's enough," Morgan said.

As she got closer I could make out her face and see she wore a tattered black dress and knee high black boots. Her black eye makeup and lipstick made her appear ghoulish. She stopped at the edge of the stage, keeping the gun aimed at the doctor.

The doctor hissed, "The abomination has something to say?"

Morgan laughed without humor. "Yeah, I have something to say. Cut him down. You sick fuckers. You can have your orgies and do your abortion thing but I'm not gonna let you kill someone who can't take part."

Lauren said, "You're just jealous!"

Morgan pointed the gun at Lauren. "Shut up, fish." She aimed the gun back at the doctor. "Wouldn't want to be a part of this if I could. But if you're offing him because he's useless to you . . . how long's it gonna be before you're after me?"

No one said anything. No one moved.

Morgan cocked the hammer on the gun. "No one has to die tonight. Let him go and we both leave. You don't kill us

... and I don't have to unload this gun on as many of you as possible." She took the few steps up to the stage. She turned to the side as she did to keep an eye on the congregation and the doctor. She pointed the gun at Nana Mary on the altar. "Come on, Nana. Up and at 'em."

Nana Mary carefully slid off the altar and onto her feet. Morgan waved the gun to insinuate the old woman should join the doctor.

"Let's go ladies," Morgan said. "Untie him."

Morgan called for Adam to help them. Adam disappeared behind the cross and the structure wobbled. I realized for the first time a ladder was located behind me. He struggled with unknotting the ropes. A part of me pitied him until it dawned on me I would face the same challenges from now on without the use of my thumbs. While Adam fumbled with my feet Morgan told Nana Mary to remove my gag.

Once I was ungagged I told the doctor I planned on killing her once I was untied.

Morgan said, "No. We're leaving."

I spat at the doctor. "Take the stupid mask off, you fucking coward."

The doctor laughed at me. Adam finally released my feet. He instructed me to grip the wood with my legs and proceeded down the ladder. My feet were thoroughly asleep and the slow return of blood made them sting.

The women began to untie my arms. Adam stood in front of me and tucked his arms under my shoulders to catch me. My face was smashed into his big greasy gut and every excruciating second that ticked by I grew angrier and angrier. I could feel my pulse in my temples and I wasn't sure if it was the effect of hanging upside down or from my anger. The ropes began to give and Adam lowered me to the floor.

The three cult members hovered over me. I rubbed the filth from my face with my bandaged hands and ignored the pain it produced. The bandage on my right hand was saturated with blood from the torn stitches. I tried to stand but my legs were wobbly and my feet were in the process of regaining blood flow. I made it to my elbows and knees. Putting pressure on my hands or feet caused too much pain. The three assholes lingering around me made me nervous.

"Get the fuck away from me!" I said.

Morgan said, "You heard him. Against the wall." She jerked the gun in the direction she wanted them to go.

Nana Mary and Adam did what she told them without hesitation. The doctor stared at Morgan for a moment before she followed the other two in a deliberately slow and defiant fashion. The townspeople shifted in their seats nervously.

"Let's go," Morgan said to me.

I made it to my feet and became lightheaded. I waited a few seconds to regain my bearings before I hobbled toward her. The pain in my feet was immense and tingled halfway up my calves. Morgan glanced at me but was overall preoccupied with keeping an eye on the others in the church.

"Can you walk?" she asked.

"What does it look like I'm doing?"

She backed her way to the wall opposite the trio, putting the congregation between us and them. She kept her back toward the wall and the gun trained on the doctor. I used the wall as a support and followed her. My feet tingled but the pain was subsiding. I was leery of the people seated in the pews closest to us. None of them were interested in getting any closer but they watched us intently. They sat motionless with the exception of their heads, which followed us silently. The masks made the townspeople's movements eerie and ominous.

Once we made it to the doors Morgan held one open for me. She kept an eye on the group as I plunged into the cold night air. The air caused goosebumps to form on my skin immediately.

Morgan stood in the doorway and directed me to get in the battered red Kia Rio parked in front of the church. The bandages on my hands made it almost impossible to open the door but I managed when I used both hands. A waft of stale cigarette smoke assaulted me when I opened the door and I knew the vehicle could be no one else's but hers.

I jumped in the passenger seat and yelled, "Come on! Come on! Come on!" I grabbed the door handle with both hands and slammed it shut.

Morgan stepped out of the doorway and ran to the car. She threw the gun in my lap when she entered the car. I was high strung and reacted like she'd thrown a venomous snake on my dick. I bucked and screamed until the gun fell onto the floorboard.

Morgan yelled, "Quit being a fucking pussy!" and started the vehicle.

She slammed the gearshift into reverse so hard I thought the lever would break. She backed out of the parking spot in a flash. She threw the car into drive without coming to a complete stop. The vehicle lurched violently as it switched gears. She punched the gas and the car almost stalled. The Rio didn't move and the engine whined.

The church door opened. Eve stepped out. Her naked body was covered in filth. She removed her mask and watched us.

Morgan looked to her and then to me. She revved the whiney engine and looked at me expectantly.

"Are we taking her or not?" Morgan asked.

Eve made no attempt to stop us or signal to join us. She stood motionless, holding her mask. The street lights made it impossible to discern her expression.

Morgan revved the engine again.

I said, "Go."

We shot into the night. I didn't turn around to see if we were followed.

19

The television remote lay on top of the motel comforter beside me. Even though I was showered I didn't think I would ever feel clean again. Lying naked on the disease infested blanket didn't bother me as much as it normally would have. I pushed the channel button with my index finger and inspected the fresh dressing Morgan applied to my hands. There didn't seem to be any fluids seeping through the material. The pain was as minimal as it was going to get with over the counter medication.

I flipped aimlessly through the stations until I came to the restricted pornography channel. I deliberated accepting the charges and jerking off while Morgan was gone. She'd been out for four hours already. I figured about the time I got going she'd come back and catch me fumbling with my cock. It would be a challenge to masturbate with my maimed hands anyway and I'd probably give up because of the pain. The last thing I wanted was to be horny and not get off. Besides, whatever the channel was showing would most likely be terrible. I wasn't some guy who got off on any pussy he laid his eyes on. As sleazy as the hotel was they'd be culprit to showing outdated seventies porn. Back when the women had bushes up to their fucking navels, halfway down their thighs, and up the cracks of their asses. Those women looked like they had sloppy, mangy beasts in place of their cunts. My dick shrank and I thought about the last porno I'd stumbled across where the women had hairy cunts and my urge to masturbate subsided.

A rustling outside the door caught my attention. Someone slipped a key into the lock. I turned the television off and covered my dick with my hand. Morgan entered with two large plastic sacks and a fast food bag. She sat the food on the desk by the door and dumped the contents of the other bags onto the second untouched bed.

I approached the pile of fabric. Morgan flopped down on the bed by my new wardrobe and lit a cigarette. I rooted out the underwear first. I clumsily tore open the package of generic boxer briefs. I never would've thought losing your thumbs would make the simplest tasks a nightmare. Once the underwear were free I pulled them on. The socks were also packaged and the next item I struggled with. The other clothing looked worn and smelled like an attic. I picked up a pair of battered boots buried below a pair of jeans, a T-shirt, a long sleeve button down shirt, and a jean jacket. All of the clothes were black or faded shades of black, contained no price tags, and were showing signs of wear.

Holding the boots up I said, "This shit's used."

She shrugged. "I only had seventy bucks. We needed gas and cigarettes and food."

I stared at her dumbfounded. "*You* need cigarettes. Not me. I need fucking clothes."

"I brought you clothes! Do you want me to take them back? Because I started at Walmart. There's no way you can get a full outfit and shoes there with twenty-five dollars." She took a pull of her smoke and blew it in my direction. "I assumed you wanted *new* underwear and a toothbrush. Who fucking cares if the other stuff's used as long as it fits? It's not like they're your permanent clothes. You're lucky I was able to find your size."

I shook the boots at her. "Someone else had these on their feet . . . with sweat and fungus and god knows what. That's disgusting."

She whined, "Oh my god." She rolled her eyes. "You have new socks!"

"I don't wear other people's clothes. It's gross."

With the cigarette still clutched in between her index and middle finger she pointed her middle finger at me and scowled. "You're a pretentious douche bag. I'm trying to help you." She waved her hands in a defensive manner. "I'm sorry I didn't have the money to buy you a new Ed Hardy shirt."

"I don't wear that garbage either."

"What a surprise."

I dropped the boots on the bed in defeat. She took a few quick hits from her smoke before crushing it out. I sighed and pulled on the T-shirt, which was too tight, and the jeans. The jeans were snug also. I struggled with the zipper and button until I figured out the best way to manage the fasteners.

I said, "What's with these pants?"

"You don't have thumbs. All pants are gonna be difficult to fasten."

"Don't antagonize me." I shifted my weight and tried to adjust the pants. "The jeans are cut weird. Are they irregulars or something?" I squatted, trying to stretch the material. "They're really tight in the thighs and around my ankles."

"They're skinny jeans."

"Are you fucking kidding me?" I looked down at the jeans and back to her. "I'm an old man! I can't wear this shit!" I snatched up the button down shirt and shook it at her. "And why is everything black? I look like a fucking hipster dumbass!"

Morgan huffed, rose, and strode over to the desk. She dug through the fast food bag and retrieved a sandwich. I whipped the bed with the shirt and cursed. She gave me a disapproving look and removed the wrapper from her sandwich.

She said, "You're a picky motherfucker for someone who's run out of options." She took a bite of the sandwich and sat on her bed. She raised a perfectly drawn eyebrow as she chewed.

I growled and continued to dress in the ridiculous clothing. My frustration level reached its peak while I fought with the buttons of the long sleeve shirt. Morgan offered to help but I snapped at her. I had to learn to do this on my own. The dusty smell of the material caused me to sneeze a few times. I tried not to think about what the clothes harbored. I wanted to take another shower. I cringed when I pulled the boots on. Morgan finished her sandwich and offered again to help with the shoelaces. I glared at her. She held her hands up in resignation. It took me five minutes to get the boots on. Suddenly the Velcro shoes the elderly wore didn't conjure the derision I would have normally given them.

I stood and held my arms out. "Are you happy? We look like a fucked up goth family."

Morgan laughed. "You may be an asshole but you're not a big enough asshole to fill my dad's shoes."

I hadn't considered the possibility Morgan might've left her family behind. We hadn't talked about what had happened or why. Our main objective was to get as far away as possible without being followed, find a place to get cleaned up and rested, and find me some clothes. I wasn't much for sympathy or deep emotional conversations. They made me feel awkward and I wanted to avoid it. All I wanted was for her to drive me to the office so I could somehow piece my life back together. She struggled to keep the hard exterior and lit another cigarette. She avoided making eye contact with me. The girl was as homeless as I was at the moment. And it sounded as if she might not have the funds to get back on her feet or a network of people to help her. If I was honest with myself I didn't give a fuck if she had daddy issues and I didn't want to hear about it for the next five hours. But she'd saved my life. The least I could do was give her a place to stay and some money until she was back on her feet.

I said, "Did, uh . . ." I rubbed the back of my neck nervously and sat on my bed facing her. I prepared myself for an onslaught of tears and emotions. "Did you leave your parents back there?"

She guffawed. "I left my parents years ago."

I fidgeted and tried to think of the next logical question to ask. "Do you have someone who can take you in?"

She squinted at me. "Take me in? Like a stray?" She laughed. "How old do you think I am?"

I shrugged. Women were touchy about their age. The young wanted to look older and the old wanted to look younger. I replied timidly. "A teenager?"

"Wait," she said. She crushed her cigarette in the ashtray and addressed me slowly. "Do you know *why* I wasn't a part of the shit happening back there?"

"Because you chose not to? I don't know. I don't even know what the fuck was happening."

She shook her head. "You poor clueless bastard."

"I mean . . . I get the gist of it. Like fucking and abortions and something to do with Satan. Yeah. I get it. They're a bunch of psychopaths. The women in town were determined to fuck me, or anyone with a dick, or even a flesh colored wall . . . except you. I figured you were underage or something. Or you didn't want to be a part of it."

"It's because the pills were formulated to stimulate the sex drive and pheromones of *women*."

I furrowed my brow. I wasn't sure where she was going with this.

She said, "I'm a transgendered woman."

My expression must have begged for a more detailed explanation.

She sighed. "I was born a man. I've transitioned into a woman. I take hormone supplements. That's how they knew about me. And it's how I found out about them. I moved to Edenville a year ago. Eventually I had to get my hormones refilled and made an appointment." She laughed. "Imagine the doc's reaction when she found out I couldn't participate in her amazing abortion race."

I scrutinized her closely, looking for signs of masculinity.

She ran her fingers along her jawline and said, "I had one of the best facial feminization surgeons in the country." She

RITUALISTIC HUMAN SACRIFICE

pulled a cigarette from the pack and tapped the butt on the table beside her bed. "They can change your forehead, eyebrows, cheeks, nose, chin and jawline, and lips. Hell, they can even shave your Adam's apple. A little lipo around the waist," she placed the cigarette in her mouth, "an augmentation of the breasts and buttocks," she lit the cigarette and exhaled, "tuck the penis into a vagina and *voila* . . . you're a girl." She placed the cigarette in her mouth and held up both hands to show me the backs of them. "But they can't do a damn thing about the hands."

Even though she had nice manicured nails painted black her hands were large and square for her petite frame. She dropped one hand and held up the cigarette with the other. She waited for a reaction from me.

I lifted my own hands briefly and said, "At least you still have thumbs."

She gave me a sympathetic half smile. "Yeah."

"And the doc left you alone?"

She shrugged. "I guess she didn't think I was a threat. I don't know why they left me alone but wanted to kill you. Dr. Paxter told me what was up at my appointment even before examining me. She promised a bunch of brainwashing horse shit. But once I told her what I was there for there wasn't a lot she could do with an inverted penis and she changed her tune. I told her if she'd give me what I wanted I wouldn't mention it to anyone." She pointed at me and said sternly, "Mind you, I wouldn't have been a part of that shit if I could've." She took a puff of her cigarette. "Bunch of sick fucks."

"Hey. You're preaching to the choir." I waited a beat. "Why did you stay around? You could've told the police."

"I just wanted my hormones. You don't know the hell my body goes through without them." She stared at the wall thoughtfully and took another pull of her cigarette. "She gave me the script and that was that. All I cared about was working my crappy job at the store and taking care of myself. I knew shit was crazy in town but I ignored it. And they ignored me. I pretty much depleted my trust fund with the surgeries and rolled into town with almost nothing. I didn't have the money to leave. And everyone in town was a part of it. Even the police." She looked at her cigarette. "I would stand outside at night and smoke and hear things. But I never stuck my nose in it . . . until last night. That was the first time I thought they might actually murder someone. I don't know what it was. I guess you can call it gut instinct."

She finished her cigarette. "I could see the church from my front door. I stepped out to smoke and saw them unload you like Hannibal Lector and wheel you into the church. Curiosity got the best of me. They'd never wheeled someone around like that. So I snuck down to the church to take a peek. By the time I made it there they were tying you to the cross. I knew I had to do something. That's how they killed Jesus, you know. I had a feeling whatever they had planned wasn't good."

I nodded.

She continued. "I ran back to get my gun. I thought I could scare the shit out of the two guys and it wouldn't be much of a big deal. But then the others started showing up. I had to wait until I knew they were all in there. I didn't want to get jumped by some late comers and . . . well . . . you were there. You know."

"Yeah," I said. "Thanks for saving my ass. I'm going to make it up to you. I want to help you until you can get a job and a new place. There's no going back, you know. And you've left everything behind. I've left everything behind. Hell, I left my wife. It seems like I should feel bad about that but I don't."

"It's just stuff. It doesn't matter. You can get a new wife. You can get a *better* wife . . . one who doesn't want to give birth to Satan."

"I think I'll stick to being a bachelor."

"You can buy new shit. Start over." She lifted her arms to display herself. "Become someone else."

"I don't think I'd take it that far."

She said, "Just sayin'." She pointed to the fast food bag.

"You should probably eat."

I nodded and did as she said. The food was cold and gross but it was better than nothing. She asked for the remote and I tossed it to her. She flipped through the channels aimlessly as I ate. When I was finished I took the new toothbrush she'd purchased to the bathroom, brushed my teeth, used the toilet, and washed my hands. She used the restroom after I did. I tried not to think about how the process of elimination worked for her since she used to be a man. Once she emerged we gathered the few items we'd acquired since our arrival— Tylenol, toothbrushes, bandages for my hands, etc.—and proceeded to the car.

The motel was located by a highway on the outer edge of a suburb. The sun was bright and the lunchtime traffic was starting to taper off. The other businesses around the motel appeared abandoned.

I glanced around to see if anyone was watching us, still paranoid we might have been followed. The other buildings didn't have any cars in their lots and the other two cars in the motel lot were here when we arrived. I slipped into the passenger's seat and Morgan sat behind the wheel.

She started the car and said, "Are you ready for your new life?"

"I feel exhausted thinking about all the stuff I'm gonna have to do."

"Don't worry," she said. "Starting over is easier than you think."

ABOUT THE AUTHOR

Loading error . . .

Other Grindhouse Press Titles

Printed in Great Britain
by Amazon

21256606R00120